CITY BY THE SHORE

FIVE STORIES, ONE CITY AND
COUNTLESS UNTOLD BATTLES

ADITYA SINHA

Clever Fox
PUBLISHING
Chennai • Bangalore

CLEVER FOX PUBLISHING
Chennai, India

Published by CLEVER FOX PUBLISHING 2025

ISBN: 978-93-7500-167-6

CONTENTS

A NOTE TO READERS

All the stories in this book are fictions, but are also a reflection of the society today. Howsoever imperfect and flawed the people are, everyone has their stories twisted in their own ways, summing up their lives.

These are not portraying the picture of perfect protagonists but rather telling stories of imperfections with which people live and mistakes they make, for life is never perfect, it's always about ups and downs, mistakes and victories, flaws and perfections.

Happy reading!

PROLOGUE

Aren't we all looking for something in our lives that is worth cherishing, so that when we close our eyes and curl up in our bed at the end of the day, we have some fond memories and people to look up to?

Sometimes I wonder looking around at all those glass windowpanes of the high-rise buildings, and think about the numerous stories that hide behind them. It's the façade that we see, and it fascinates us, but underneath there is a whole different world where people are shrieking out inaudibly to feel someone by their side, to hold their hand, to pour their heart out or to rescue them from the harsh realities they are living in.

Life is merely a collection of memories and experiences that occur, and one can never say it is going to be perfect by the end of the day. It's the ups and downs that makes it interesting and worth fighting for. It's our hope for a better tomorrow that really counts and makes us who we are.

Everyone of us are fighting our demons inside, for all of us have something or the other that keeps us awake at night.

Well, you know, life is too short, so it's better to open your eyes and start doing the things you feel passionate about, start expressing your feelings to the ones you love, and start living the life the way you want, for life is too short to give up on your own happiness.

THE INEVITABLE RACE

Karan

It was 8:30 in the morning when I received another e-mail. I had been awake for the last three hours and still wasn't done with the morning chores. Being a freelance software developer wasn't easy, that too with a full-time job. The client's demands are never-ending, and you just have to dig up your head for every diminutive issue, troubleshooting for hours.

I dressed up and started for my office, it was a forty-minute ride from my apartment. Honestly, whichever big car I would dream to own, commuting by bike in Mumbai had always been better, as it easily saves an hour each day.

I was stuck at a traffic signal when I realised it was 9:30 already, and the stock market was open. The traders would be howling right now, calling their shots at the dips and buying a bulk of stocks. I tried to convince myself to wait, but my urge to check my portfolio performance was eating me from inside. I checked the traffic signal, it was red and showed 92 seconds as the waiting time before it turned green.

I pulled out my phone. Sensex was down, and well, most of my stocks' values had fallen abruptly. I just sat there disappointed, scrolling through the green and red numbers on my phone's screen when I heard people honking and howling from behind. The traffic signal had turned green, and I was holding up the traffic behind me. I somehow hurried the phone back into my pocket and accelerated as fast as I could.

It was eight in the evening and I had just packed up from the gym and was headed back to my apartment. After the whole day of office, travel, and then the gym I hardly got time for myself, though whatever was left of the day, I spent it on enhancing my skills and learning new stuffs. I believed that life is too short to live and die mediocre.

I didn't belong to a family with means, but I had always had big dreams since I was a child. Though lately, I realised that time was slipping fast, and now was the time to give my best to chase those dreams. I had always believed that there is nothing that one cannot achieve. It's just one's perspective on life and success that makes one capable.

I had been trying hard to be the best version of myself. I was grinding at the gym for the perfect physique. I worked my way from my last terrible job to a better one, my present one, but I still wasn't satisfied. I started freelancing and stock trading, which still didn't feel enough.

I didn't know if this urge to be better and richer was good or not, but all I knew was, that all the dreams that I had once as a child still felt far away, and now was my only chance to work towards them.

I heard my phone vibrating while I was clicking keys on my keyboard. It was my dad.

"*Hey, dad. How's everything at home*?"

"*Everything's great, you tell. How are you?*"

"*How's your job going?*" He asked.

"*It's fine. It's going well.*" I replied.

"*That's nice. You know I just got to hear that Mehra uncle's son is going to the USA next month. He got a job there.*" He told me sounding very heartily.

Before I could respond he added "*and your cousin Ashish, he got another job now, they are going to pay him 40 LPA.* "He sounded excited telling me the accomplishments of the ones whom he cared about.

And there I was, a disappointment to my parents, still earning less than half of that, still not having achieved much.

After a few more minutes of conversation and catching up, the call got disconnected. I sat there staring at the screen of my mobile phone, struck on the fact that everyone around me, even the younger ones were doing far better than me. I was just a loser trying to convince myself that my paycheques were enough.

I sat down at my desk and started clicking keys on my laptop again trying to solve an algorithm. That was part of my daily schedule now. After all, I was preparing for my dream job, to get into top product-based companies. Well, it wasn't just mine, it's a dream of every software graduate to work for these Silicon Valley companies.

I kind of felt that it was my only way to climb several steps at once and maybe surpass my peers who were earning twice what I did.

After spending almost forty-five minutes stuck in front of my laptop, I knew today wasn't the day. I had a lot of things on my mind, and I was missing even the smallest errors in the code, which made me feel even more like a loser. I shut my laptop and walked out of the room.

I pulled a bottle of whiskey, a glass and sat there on the balcony, playing Prateek Kuhad in the background, sipping down the drinks alone and watching the city that lay in front of me.

The best part of living on the 17th floor was the mesmerising view that I had for myself. I sat there enjoying the cold breeze, while my drink numbed me down slowly. I just kept looking at the high-rise buildings that stood afar and some distant flickering lights on top, wondering what stories were concealed behind those huge window panes.

AARTI

"*Mom, I am leaving for college. I have kept the medicine on the table, please have it.*" I hugged her, and walked out. I had to catch the local train to my college. The station was almost half a kilometre away. It didn't seem quite far as it took me just four songs to reach there. Well, that was part of my daily schedule, and so I knew it well. I had a playlist that played every day on a loop.

It's Mumbai, the city where millions come trying their luck to live the life of their dreams. Just a few get to have a taste of it and the rest are just crushed in the chaos of this fast-paced city, and by the time they realise it, it's too late. People bet their lives, gambling to leave their footprints in this city, but this city has a different way of selection. Just like the shore washes off most of the things, so does this city.

Here, I was, rushing to catch the local train. Somehow for that exact moment, my only goal was just to board the train and get enough space to stand in the jam-packed ladies' coach. I had been living my life working for bits and pieces.

Looks like my day was going pretty well. I got a seat so can't complain. It was almost an hour's journey to my college. I pulled out notes from my bag and started going through the highlighted lines and marked paragraphs.

I was studying in one of the best colleges in Mumbai. Well, my academics got me there, but surviving the college was no less of a challenge than completing the whole syllabus in a day. People were crazy here. Drugs, weed, making out in the back of some building was something you could see every day, all you needed to know was the right place.

"*Hey, Aarti!*" Somebody tapped on my shoulder as I took my seat for the lecture.

"*Hey Rohit, wassup?*" I replied as I made space for him.

"*Looks like we are early today.*" He commented with a smirk as our professor entered the lecture hall.

Rohit was a good friend of mine, or maybe I could say the only one. I was one of the loner students. It was not like I didn't like to be around people, but I just liked my company better, and certainly, a good taste in music got me a little aloof. Rohit and I got to know each other just a month back, but somewhere I felt I knew him for much longer.

I was preparing for Chartered Accountancy and pursuing graduation in Commerce. My father was into finance and so I always had a taste for it. He wanted me to become a doctor, but I loved playing with numbers.

I was again on the local train, standing, clenching my fingers around the hook just to make sure I don't lose balance and fall. Just a usual evening with my earphones on and loud music playing. The college was over and I was heading home.

"*Maa, please come and eat. Dinner is ready,*" I said as I saw her lying on the bed, still, with her eyes open staring outside the window.

"*Maa,*" I went to her and sat by her side.

"*Maa,*" I said again, as I shook her slowly. She looked at me with her heavy eyes.

"*Maa, it's been one year now. Please don't do this to yourself. It won't change anything.*"

"*Please maa, you need to take care of yourself.*" I said as she sat there leaning on me, with her face lying on my shoulder. I felt my voice breaking, I paused.

I held her and walked her to the dining table.

"*Maa, you know I had a great day at college. Today it was really funny when we pulled a prank on one of our professors.*" I said and narrated everything that happened the whole day, told her all the funny incidents just to see her smile. I kept talking till the time she ate her dinner, which was barely a chapati.

"*Maa, you have lost your appetite, are you on a diet, huh*?" I tried to crack another one as I realised, she was going to leave the plate half full again, just like every day for the last year.

She looked at me, got up, and walked to her bed again, the same way she did every day. I just looked at her, walking away and lying on the bed, staring at the ceiling, just like every other day.

I sat there as my lips dried up, and a tear ran down my cheek. I just left my plate there, barely finishing my dinner, and ran into my room. I locked the room and curled myself up to the pillow as tears ran down, and I couldn't stop no matter how hard I tried. Maybe today was the day I just had to let it go, all the pain that I was holding on to, that had burdened me for a long time.

My dad died last year, and to this day my mom has not been able to pull herself together. I still feel as if it was just yesterday when we were all together and everything was just perfect. I still can't believe how quickly everything changed in our lives. Since dad died my mom has been on meds. She barely sleeps, barely walks, and doesn't even talk much. She just sits staring outside the window. It has been weeks since she left the apartment. I try my best to hold myself together as now I am the one who needs to take care of her.

I had been trying hard, really hard to be strong, to hold her every time she needs me, but I was done pretending that I was alright. After everything that happened, I was just carrying a fake façade pretending to be strong enough to take care of everything, but I was not. Sometimes I felt that I needed a shoulder to cry on, to tell what I had been going through. I could never say anything to my mom, I had to keep myself together in front of her as she was already shattered.

Karan

"Hey Karan, a moment please?" Mr. Srivastava tapped on my shoulder as I turned around. He walked to his cabin signalling me to follow him.

I went inside, it was a large room with AC running at significantly low temperature. I pulled down my sleeves trying hard to pretend that the cold air wasn't already biting me. I sat down on the chair he gestured to, while he took his seat on the other side of the table, facing me.

"*So, Karan. How's the work going?*" He asked, leaning forward and looking at me sharply.

"It's going good," I said. I suspected that he wanted to know about details, so I continued, *"I have completed most of the modules that I was assigned to work on."*

"There's just one left. We have a meeting about it tomorrow, and once the requirements are finalised, I'll start working on it right away." I explained, detailing my task schedules.

"*Great Karan, I am proud to see you performing really well.*" He said as he peeked into his phone.

I looked at him, glancing on his mobile phone and then switching to the laptop, again and again.

"*Well, the appraisals are here Karan and as well as the promotions. You have performed consistently in all the quarters, so I am hoping that something good is coming your way.*" He broke the silence as he locked his phone and kept it away.

"*And this time we are planning to have the annual event in Lonavala so that it can be a short vacation for each of us as well. The bookings have already been made, it's in the coming weekend.*" He added further.

I looked at him as he pursed his lips, peeked at his phone again, looked like he had an e-mail open.

"*Karan, I will just need you to work on one more assignment. It's a small task, it won't take much of your time. Actually, one of the developers who was working on that module has called in sick, and there is no other responsible soul that I can trust except for you. Could you please look into it?*" He asked.

I looked at him, scrolling through the mail again. I already had enough work on my plate, but I wasn't sure if this was the time to let it pass, because the promotions and appraisals were close.

"*Sure, I can work on that. I am just working on one of the modules. I will complete that, and then I can start working on this one.*" I replied still wondering what the new work is going to be. Needless to say, analysing someone else's code was no less of a pain.

"*Karan, you will need to complete it today. I have mailed you the details. Please complete it today and update me before you leave.*" He replied. I saw him clicking some keys on his laptop. Well, there was no way out now.

"*Sure, I will.*" I said as I stood up and started walking towards the door.

"*It's going to be a fun weekend Karan, prepare well.*" He smiled with his thumbs up. I nodded and walked out of the cabin.

"*Hey, Karan! Mr. Employee of the year.*" Sanya giggled as she saw me coming out of Mr. Srivastava's cabin.

"*Oh c'mon*" I laughed.

"*I am not kidding. Everybody around here knows about you. You have been here just for a year and have pulled the project from scratch till here. It's pretty obvious you're going to get it.*" She pulled a chair and sat beside me as I turned on my laptop to check my e-mail.

"*Let's see, we can't say much about it.*" I replied.

Somewhere deep down I knew I deserved it and I had a feeling that I might be the one, but I never knew for sure and thus never preferred admitting it, even to myself.

It was 9:30 at night and I was still working. The code I received had several bugs, and I wondered how someone thought that it could be production-ready in such a state. I had been working for six straight hours, sipping down mugs of coffee, digging my brain out to solve the bugs.

I was finally done with the code and the documentation. It was already 11:30 p.m. I mailed the update to Mr. Srivastava and left for the day.

I just rode off on the glittering roads of Mumbai. After finishing all the work for the day, the only thing that was stuck in my mind were the appreciations that I had been receiving lately. I was glad that I was being recognised for my contribution to the organisation. It was nothing like my old job, it didn't suck for sure. I had just completed my first year in this organisation and it seemed to be treating me well.

It was Saturday morning. I was supposed to leave for Lonavala with my office mates. The whole team was going by a traveller, but I told them that I will be coming by bike. I wanted a break from the chaos. A bike ride from

Mumbai to Lonavala wasn't really a bad idea, especially for a quiet solo ride.

Riding through the range of tunnels, and in between the hills wasn't a bad idea at all. Honestly, I was loving it. The ride was almost three hours long, but along the scenic landscapes around the road, I lost the track of the time.

Howsoever hectic your week is, some good corporate-funded resort with free drinks on a weekend makes it feel worth it. It was almost dark, and we were ready for the event, which was going to start in the next half an hour.

Beer, snacks, and some scotch, were spread across the hall. We were seated in a large hall with hundreds of chairs lined up. Then there were the VPs, Directors, and the Chief Officers seated in the first row by the stage. The event was midway already. There was our GM addressing the employees and sharing the details of the company's performance over the last few quarters.

It was already 8 and I was just waiting for the event to get over so that I could serve myself some chicken and scotch on the rocks. The perfect combination for me, a spicy platter and a drink to soothe the mind and pour the heart out.

I pulled out my phone, it was vibrating. It was a call from a friend. I started walking to the end of the hall and found a quiet place.

"*Hey bro, wassup?*" I asked as I took a seat in a corner.

"*Karan, did you check the news right now? I have sent you the link.*" He sounded completely astounded.

I had no clue whatever was going on. I put my phone on speakers and clicked the link that he had sent. I was staggered as I scrolled through the article.

"*What the hell?*" I almost shouted as I scrolled further.

"*Bro, please calm down. It's going to be fine, let's wait until Monday.*" I heard him speaking from the other side of the phone.

I sat there speechless, staring at my mobile's screen. I disconnected the call.

I started reading the article again. The company's stock, on which I had invested most of my savings in, had just declared themselves bankrupt. It was Saturday and the market was closed, but I knew on Monday it was going to be a blood bath.

I received a few more messages from him about the details. I switched off my mobile and rushed inside the hall again. I was sweating and my face had gone pale. I took a seat and wiped my face with a napkin, I was getting restless. I just sat there trying to keep my head straight, waiting for the announcement to happen. The award for the Employee of The Year was going to be awarded, and that was my only hope for the day.

It's been almost half an hour since the speech was still going on and every employee was waiting desperately for it to end.

Well, it finally ended, and there was the CTO on the stage to announce the winner of the award. There were cheers from all around the place.

I felt a tap on my shoulder. It was Sanya. "*So, where are you going to treat me for this?*"

She looked at me, I was pale and sweating. "*What happened Karan? Are you okay?*" She asked.

"*Don't be nervous, it's going to be you. That's a sure thing.*" She held my hand as she tried to comfort me.

"*Thanks!*" That's all I could say.

And then the announcement started. "*The employee of the year award goes to*", the whole of the hall was in a pin drop silence. I could hear my heart racing.

"*Anirudh*" The voice echoed in the hall loudly. I looked up to the stage again for the confirmation. Yes, he was walking by to the stage. Sanya merely shouted, "*What the hell is this?*" I was in shock. I just sat there staring at the stage. It was yet another big disappointment for me. I just stood up from my seat and walked past the crowd. I took two beer bottles and walked out of the hall.

It was empty. I could hear the noise from the inside of the hall. Few of them celebrating and rest of them consoling themselves to be better the next time, though they knew they wouldn't even try. And here I was, who gave almost everything to my work and now here I was, again a loser.

I walked to the back of the building. The waiters and caterers were preparing the stalls of food, and at one far end, there was a big pool with a hillside view.

I walked up to the pool and took a seat in a corner. It was calm and soothing, away from all the chaos and noise, with an enchanting view of the town behind. I cracked open the beer and had a sip. It felt better being away from the known faces that would walk to me with their sympathies. I was fine alone; I knew I lost again.

Maybe I was just a loser trying too hard to be in the race of winners, not knowing my place well.

Aarti

It was yet another day. I woke up, prepared breakfast, got my mom to eat and have the medicine, and then left for college. As I didn't get a seat on the train, I had to go through my playlist again. I was sick of the playlist by now, but experimenting with new songs was difficult. I really needed to sit and explore some new tracks and give them time to actually settle in. Well, I had it planned for the weekend.

"*Hey, prepared for the weekend?*" Rohit asked as he slammed his bag on the desk. He took the seat next to me.

"*What's this weekend?*" I asked in surprise. I knew he had plans almost every weekend but I wasn't really a part of them; the partying, road trips, and all.

"*Really, what?*" I asked him as I saw him going through some messages on his mobile.

"*We were discussing it on the Whatsapp group last night, didn't you see?*" Rohit stared at me and then continued, "*Oh well, I forgot. You must have put it on mute. Isn't it?*" He asked with his brows raised.

I nodded slowly and giggled.

"*We are going to Lonavala next weekend, and before you say no, it's a departmental event, so everyone has to go,*" he stated, as he pulled the phone from my hand and showed me the message.

"*I can't leave mom alone*" I told him, trying to convince him. Although somewhere I knew this wasn't going to work this time. I had been avoiding all the get-togethers for a long time now, and gradually people stopped asking me to be a part of them anymore.

"*I understand that Aarti, but not this time, please. This is the one outing where all of us are going to be there.*" "*Pleaseeee!!!*" Rohit said, putting all the efforts to convince me.

"*It's just for a day with an overnight stay, we will be back the very next morning.*" He added.

"*Okay fine, I will talk to my mom about it,*" I replied with a giggle as I saw him literally pleading.

"*Well, I am considering it as a 'YES'.*"

"*Sure,*" I replied.

It was Saturday morning and we had already started for Lonavala. I had to call a neighbour and ask her to look after mom and give her medicines on time, as I knew mom would not even bother to take them. The bus was packed with the students of our department. It was a two-hour journey from Mumbai. We were supposed to start early in the morning but with so many people coming from different parts of the city, it was already 11. I had a window seat with my earphones plugged in, away from everyone, which was kind of perfect for me. People were dancing, playing cards, and doing everything else apart from being glued to their seats, and I was least interested in joining them.

We reached at 2 in the afternoon. The traffic in the city was worse, and it took us almost one hour just to get to the suburbs. There was a huge resort booked for us, one that could easily accommodate several medium-sized parties. There was also a huge pool in front of it.

We were almost 30 and had shared rooms for three. The resort was good and the view from the pool was undoubtedly amazing.

We spent the whole day exploring around, engaging in chit chats, and then in the evening had sports events and functions. There were a few dance performances and band performance and then our Dean addressed us. Summing up the whole thing, it was just fine, except for the resort, of course, which was marvellous.

It was 8:00 and the party had already started. Music was loud and the place was glimmering, and almost everyone had a drink in hand. I could see some couples making out in the corner.

"*Hey, c'mon, join us for a drink.*" Rohit handed me a beer as he saw me standing in one corner.

"*I am not really in a mood yaar,*" I responded, putting the beer back on the table.

"*C'mon, not today. I never ask you to drink but today you have to.*" Rohit started again, popping open the beer bottle.

"*Okay, fine. Just one beer, nothing more.*" I said and took a sip.

"*How many have you already had?*" I asked as I saw him taking unsteady steps. He held a glass, which looked like whiskey.

"*Ahh, not much. I just got done with the starters. The main course has just started Aarti.*" He said as he drank the whole drink in one go.

"*Rohit, you need to keep a check, don't do this.*" I held him, trying to stop him from taking another drink from the bar.

"*C'mon, Aarti*" He screamed childishly.

I was just going to pull Rohit when some of his friends came and made him take three neat shots.

Damn it, I will have to pick him up, he is going to get wasted. I stood there watching him. The very next moment I saw him walking right to the centre of the garden by the bar, trying to walk straight along the line. It was hilarious. His only goal was to walk straight along the gap of the marbles spread on the floor, and he was barely able to do that.

After almost half an hour of the drama, Rohit came back to me, and he was drunk as fuck.

"*Hey, I want to talk to you about something?*" Rohit asked as he dragged me to one corner.

"*Rohit, are you okay? What happened?*" I asked him in surprise. He was acting weird.

"*I just needed to tell you something.*" He said as he pushed me to the wall.

"*Rohit, what the hell are you doing?*" I snapped at him, as he got closer.

"*It's just...*" He started and then leaned in to kiss me.

I was petrified and shocked. I pushed him away without a thought and the next moment my hand flew up and I slapped him.

I just froze, having no idea what to do. Rohit stood there, shocked. I was flabbergasted. I didn't mean to slap him, it just happened. I didn't even know if I had overreacted, but I knew for sure that I didn't like what he did, and that was totally wrong.

"*Really, Aarti, how can you fucking slap me, you fraud?*" Rohit shouted at me.

And then happened, the only thing I was afraid of. We had all the attention from everyone around us. I was still surprised by whatever just happened, and in just a second all the eyes were on us, from every corner.

I wanted to say sorry and make everything alright. I knew he was drunk, and he didn't mean it.

"*What the hell are you talking about? Rohit, please calm down.*" I tried to soothe him. Whatever he said, I didn't care at that moment. I knew he was a good friend of mine.

"*Ohh c'mon, everybody has to know who you are.*"

"*Hello, peeps, in case you don't know who she is… Well, nobody knows who she is, let me do you all a favour. She is the daughter of Rakesh Singhania.*"

He continued as I just stood there dumbstruck, scared of what was about to unfold.

"*In case you don't remember the name, let me remind you all. Don't you remember the businessman, millionaire, sorry, the fraud businessman who was charged with a felony just a year ago when he faked his own death to claim the money from his insurance.*"

"*C'mon, still can't remember.*" He shouted looking around at everyone.

All the eyes were glued to me now. I could hear some whispers around me. I just stood there, ashamed, shocked, betrayed, I don't know how I felt but I was shattered. I left the place and ran away, without even turning back. I just wanted to hide somewhere and to be never be found, I just needed to be alone. I never felt so disgusted ever in my life.

It was almost half an hour since I was crying locked in the restroom. I was still trying to catch my breath as everything just came back in a flashback, and it felt like it all just happened yesterday.

I walked past the pool to an empty, secluded spot. I settled myself in a corner, trying to hide myself from the world around me. I sat there aghast, staring at the hills that laid in front of me, and the far off scanty glimmering lights that draped the village in sheets of serenity.

WHEN THEY MET

"*Hey, you okay?*" Karan asked as he saw Aarti sitting in the corner, just a few steps away from him with her face buried in her palms, legs folded.

She nodded, with her face still buried.

"*Want a beer?*" Karan asked, pulling out a bottle.

"*It might help.*" He added, as he slid the bottle towards her.

Karan just sat there admiring the serene view. The stars gleaming, enveloping the sky above, and the flickering lights on a distant hill.

Karan heard the beer bottle click from beside him. He saw her pick up the bottle, and take a sip.

"*Thanks! Kinda needed it.*" She sighed as she turned towards Karan.

"*What's your story?*" Aarti asked him,

"*I am sure, there is something, otherwise you wouldn't end up sitting here, alone, away from the party.*" Aarti added, looking at Karan.

"*Well, where should I start? I would say I had a crappy day, but I don't know whom to blame, the day or me.*" Karan sighed as he engulfed a large sip out of the beer bottle.

"*Really, what went wrong?*" Aarti asked as she took another sip.

"*Ummm… there is a party going on over there.*" Karan said as he pointed towards the other side of the resort.

He took a pause, another sip, and started.

"*For this particular day, I had been putting my best into my work, to be the best employee of the year. I had everything planned. The perfect hike, an early promotion, my career growth, but well, I ended up here.*" Karan poured out everything he had been holding onto.

"*Well, it doesn't really end here. There is another one.*" Karan said, sipping down the whole bottle in one go.

"*The company in which I had invested most of my savings just declared itself bankrupt...*" Karan paused, as he took a deep breath. "*Everything is just falling apart.*"

"*And you know the worst part is, the plans, I had ever framed, have failed me, just every freaking time. I honestly just don't know what to do anymore.*"

The pause followed, as they both sat there, pouring the drink down, letting the reality hit, one moment at a time.

Aarti finally broke the silence.

"*I understand that's a huge loss, but don't worry that's not the end of the world.*" She mumbled.

"*Really, for you, it might not be.*" Karan almost shouted at her.

"*You have no idea how hard I have worked for all of this. This job and everything didn't just come to me. I was grinding my ass in some shitty company last year. I worked hard.*" Karan rambled/rumbled pouring out his anger. Aarti was staring at him, a bit surprised.

"After a freaking 10 - 12 hour work day, I work on side projects and freelance so that I can make more money. I have been upskilling, learning investing and trading. I have been literally grinding like a machine for I don't know how long now, and when things end like this, it feels like all of it was for nothing."

"*Sometimes I wonder if whatever I do is even worth it. You know I have lost my social life. All I do is work and work. I don't remember when I last went clubbing, or to a party, or on a road trip. I have compromised everything just for one thing, success, and it has always kicked me in my nuts.*"

He had it bottled up, and he let it go, all of it. He poured out everything.

"*I am really sorry, I said all of this to you. We don't even know each other.*" He said as he looked at Aarti staring at him.

"*That's okay. You needed to let it out.*" Aarti replied with a smile.

"*I guess so,*" Karan replied. "*I am sorry, I kind of shouted.*" He apologised again.

"*That's okay, don't worry*" Aarti replied.

"*Although, what I have learnt is that plans rarely work, just live in the moment. Life is always going to crumble them when you least expect it.*" She added.

He nodded.

"*Don't you think if it were so simple most of us would be living the best lives?*" Aarti said, gulping another sip.

Karan nodded.

"*By the way, I am Karan.*" he introduced himself, as he kept his empty beer bottle to the side.

"*Oh, I am Aarti.*"

"*Should I get another round of beers?*" Karan asked as he saw her bottle almost empty.

"*Sure!*" Aarti took the last sip and handed him the empty bottle.

Karan walked to the counter on the other side of the pool and got four pints of beer.

"*Woww, four pints. Planning to get drunk?*" Aarti giggled as she saw Karan carrying four bottles.

"*I guess I need to be in a bit of a blur. Staying drunk is better for me, for today at least.*" He laughed as he sat beside Aarti.

"*This looks beautiful, doesn't it?*" Aarti said, pointing at the small town that lay on the foothills, far off.

"*Yeah, it's serene. Feels like a perfect night, lovely place, amazing view*" Karan added, as he handed her a pint.

"*Beer's making it even better, I guess.*" Aarti laughed as she took the first sip.

"*Undoubtedly!*" Karan chuckled.

"*What's your story Aarti? A pretty girl sitting here, away from the college party?*"

"*Ahhh, are you hitting on me? Really?*" She laughed as she asked Karan.

"*Ummm... wait, am I?*" Karan chuckled as he took another sip from his bottle.

"*What is it, about you? feel like there is a lot you're hiding behind that smile.*" Karan asked looking into her eyes.

There was a meagre pause, and then Aarti spoke.

"*It's a long story, you wouldn't want to spoil your hangover.*" She told Karan curling her lip slightly.

"*Don't worry we have enough booze tonight, after all my company is paying.*" Karan replied with a chuckle.

"*And I guess we have all time as well unless you have to go somewhere.*" He added.

"*Well,*" Aarti took a deep breath. "*Wondering where I should start ?*" She added.

Karan was still looking at her, glancing at her scrolling through the thoughts that were running in her mind.

"*Ummm... my dad*" She stumbled over the words. Her eyes were shining in the dark, and her voice got heavy. Karan brushed her hand firmly with his palm. She nodded with a faint smile.

"*I was living in the UK, pursuing my graduation from one of the best universities there. My dad and mom were in Mumbai. My dad was a businessman.*" She paused.

"Everything was different back then. We were happy, I used to come to Mumbai often to visit them. It was one of the best days of my life."

"We were rich, quite actually. My dad had a few sea-facing apartments in Mumbai, quite a few luxury cars and more importantly we were living a great life. We were happy." She continued…

"I was away, but I used to talk to them every day. Though I guess being away was the worst part as I didn't know what was happening back here in India. My father got into some business troubles that I wish I knew about then. By the time I got to know about everything, it was too late." Karan looked at her hand, it was trembling, and her voice shaking.

She continued…

"When I came back to India, I got to know that he had lost almost all of his business. Although mom and dad didn't want me to know any of this but when I did get to know how bad it was, I decided to drop off from my college and come back to India. Of course, it was the last thing they wanted but I had to. They had to sell most of the properties, and the cars. We moved to a small 2BHK apartment with whatever we were left with."

Karan looked at her. Her eyes were moist, breaths heavy. Of course, he couldn't do much, he just leaned further and held her hand delicately.

"*It was not over yet. Just after three months, we got to know that somebody filed a case against dad for some offence in the business that he didn't even commit.*" Her voice was breaking. She just sat there embracing the pause in between, that let her breathe amply.

She gathered the courage again, took a deep breath, and started. "*Whatever he had left, he had to put almost every penny into that case, he even had to take loans. Things got worse and then one day…*" She said collecting the words together, and then there was another pause, a long one.

Karan looked at her. Her lips were dry, pursed together, her hands were shivering with the cold breeze. Before Karan could say anything, she broke into tears. Karan wanted to comfort her to the best he could, but he knew she had a lot inside and she needed to let it go that night. Karan held her as he saw tears pouring out of her eyes.

"*Aarti, calm down. Everything will be fine.*" Karan whispered as he held her by her shoulders.

"*Nothing's fine Karan, nothing's fine. Everything was ruined that day.*" Karan held her tightly by her shoulders as she was crying continuously.

"*Dad never came back that night, he never came back.*" She just fell apart on his shoulders.

"*Aarti...*" Karan just sat there holding her tight.

"*Till today I call the police station just to check in case they found him. They couldn't even trace...*"

"*his body...*" Her words were breaking. She was crying her heart out.

"*And now, people blame him for faking his death to get the insurance money.*"

"*How could one say that? I wonder how fucked up people are to even think of it.*" She mumbled slowly in her broken voice with her face lying on Karan's shoulder.

Karan was taken aback by what he just heard. It took him a while to let it sink in. He sat there wondering the ways in which life messes up people. All he could think was how messed up things can be for people but still they have to wake up everyday, walk out the door, carry a facade, faking it the whole time. How pretentious one has to be, canvassing a smile, all over their face, while everything is falling apart in their life.

All his life he had been running around for money that meant everything to him, and there was this girl, in his arms, who once had everything that he had ever dreamt of, but now it meant nothing to her.

Aarti made herself comfortable after a while, her face was still covered with the marks of tears.

"*I am sorry.*" She sighed as she took another sip from the beer.

"*You don't need to be, I am glad you talked.*" Karan hugged her with his arms wrapped around her shoulders.

They both sat there watching the clouds move and the wind whistle. The night was long, and they had a lot to talk about. They found someone to share their stories about dreams, desires, and sorrows in the name of a stranger.

Sometimes life's greatest gift to us could be a complete stranger, who just might stay by our side, and listen to us, no matter how broken or shattered we are.

Life's too short for carefully laid plans that crumble anyway. Sometimes all we can do is step into the moment and live it fully, because that's what stays with us till the end.

THE YEARS BETWEEN US

KSHITIJ

Sitting in the café staring at the screen of my MacBook, I took another sip of the americano, it was already cold and there was barely any left. I went to the counter and ordered one more and walked out of the cafe, stood at the façade looking at the bustling street down. I started the playlist on my phone with my ear buds on.

I walked back to my table, took my seat, and looked around. In a small, confined place I could see a story brewing on every table.

On my left was an elderly couple sitting, holding hands and giggling. It was beautiful, looking at a simple yet pure love. They looked happy together. It was the forever type of love that people long for, growing old together, being there for each other, till the end of time.

On the next table sat a guy, wheatish-complexioned, patchy beard and ruffled hair, which he kept smoothing nervously with his hands. And there sat a girl next to him, beautiful eyes, curly hair, and a smile that could actually heal people. She had her legs crossed, in a fern-coloured dress, which complemented her skin perfectly. I could see the guy fumbling, smiling nervously at times, clearly nervous to express himself. On the other hand, the girl was lost in her own world, reciting her story wholeheartedly, laughing, tucking her hair at the back of her ears, totally unaware that she was making the guy fall in love with her every passing second.

"*Wish you luck brother, I have a feeling it's not going to end well.*" I murmured to myself looking at the guy. I am sure most of us have been at this point somewhere in our lives.

On the table opposite mine sat a lady by herself with no laptop, no book, and not even a phone. She was sipping her coffee while eating a croissant. She looked beautiful, was definitely older, maybe in her early 40s, but looked amazing for her age. Her curly hair with burgundy highlights on the sides looked perfect. There sat a Coach tote bag beside her, she definitely looked like the SOBO (South Bombay) types.

"*Well, she has a book.*" She took one out from her bag, and it was the classic as I would call it, "Eleven Minutes" by Paulo Coelho.

"*Interesting read!*" I muttered, as Priya put down the coffee cup on my table along with two napkins. I knew her name; having been a regular here for the past few months, I actually knew almost everyone working here.

It had become sort of a hobby of mine to look at people and try to figure out their stories. I believe each one of us has stories worth telling, but we all are just too busy untying knots of the chaos in our lives and we often forget that we are the protagonists, and we should live like one.

I have been working on my book for a while. It's been two months and I have not been able to move past the first three chapters. Every time I re-read, my thoughts shuffle among the plethora of ideas, and I ended up re-writing again. This was a vicious cycle that kept me running the same mile again and again and I was unable to decide upon the best plot line.

I always wanted to be a writer but with college and then job, something always came up, and I could never complete the manuscript. I started multiple times but it always came to a halt.

Sitting long hours in the cubicle every day, working through the presentations and late night client calls, I was not left with enough energy to sit back and work on the book. It needed a different mind space which I was totally devoid of.

Buzzing alarms to traffic honking, clicking keyboards to Teams caller tune, numerous redundant meetings throughout the day and coming home around midnight, that is what my day looked like.

With every passing day I could feel time slipping away, with me being at the centre of the chaos just living day to day, like being ground in a machine with tailored instructions.

Finally, I took a leap of faith and decided to go on sabbatical. I knew it wasn't going to be easy as there were a lot of questions, confusions and doubts. Will I be able to utilize the time to the fullest? How am I going to manage six months without pay? How much savings of mine is going to get drained? Will the book actually work, do I have it in me to write a bestseller? There are many debut writers who are lost in the crowd, will I be just another one? I had so many questions, but not enough answers. All I knew was I didn't want to have regrets later in life. If I didn't try, I will never know if I was good at it, or if it was ever meant for me. So, I had to give it a shot for myself.

Kanika

"Mum, here's the shopping list, I need all of these."

I looked at the long list that Anya handed me. I liked the fact that she anticipated almost everything that she would need for her hostel life, from Maggie packets to towels and night gowns. It was a long list.

"Sure, I will be heading to the market in a bit, I will get all these." I replied.

I went to the other room, turned on my laptop and started checking my emails, LinkedIn or Naukri.com, to see if I had gotten any responses from any of the job applications. Unfortunately, there were none. There were some automatic rejection emails from companies that I had applied to.

I sat there staring at the screen. I switched to another tab on the browser, which showed the fee structure of Anya's college. I scrolled through, staring at the numbers. It was big enough to consume almost half of my monthly salary.

"Mum, I have texted you a few more things, please get them as well." Anya barged into the room, scrolling through her mobile phone.

I was done with the shopping. I checked the list again to make sure I got everything and I had. It was not at all easy moving around the mall, carrying numerous shopping bags hanging on my shoulders and a few dangling from my fingers too. I finally reached the parking lot and dumped everything in the trunk of my car.

I started the car, turned on the AC and sat there for a few minutes looking at the bills, all of them laid out. I opened the calculator app on my phone and started tapping on the screen. The sum totalled to Rs 25,000.

"*Damn, that's a dent!*" I said to myself as I kept the bills aside in my bag.

I was happy that Anya got into a good college for her graduation, she had been putting a lot of effort in her studies and it had finally paid off.

Living with a single parent hasn't been easy for her especially in her teen years. It's been seven years since my husband and I separated. Sometimes I feel like it was just yesterday when we were all together, laughing, playing, like any other happy family.

For Anya, it was devastating when she came to know about our separation. It fell on my shoulders to tell her about it, and it wasn't easy. I had several sleepless nights, re-arranging the words so as to make her understand without hurting her, but no matter how hard I tried, how many attempts I made, it still hurt her deeply.

I knew she had numerous questions to ask, but she kept them to herself, so as as not to put me in a position where I would have to relive everything. She knew it would hurt me. I wish I could make her understand that it's just life and it was no one's fault. Sometimes some relationships just turn bitter with time, and for the sake of your own happiness, you need to let go of people. Otherwise, it starts eating you from inside and you are just left with hate for each other.

KSHITIJ MEETS KANIKA

I got up from my chair again. The cup was empty and so were my thoughts. I leaned on the grill, shut my eyes, and took a deep breath.

I stood there, letting all the thoughts in, all the sounds of chaos in, not fighting anything. With my muddled mind and eyes shut, I tried imagining my protagonist and started shaping the storyline.

I heard a thud from behind. I opened my eyes, there was the lady, the one who sat opposite to me. She had dropped her book . She had a cigarette in one hand and was picking up the book with the other.

"*I hope the smoke isn't bothering you,*" she said, brows arched, a thin curl of smoke leaving her lips as she took another puff.

"Don't worry, I'm used to passive smoke," I replied with a grin. "*Surrounded by smokers all my life, I've had my fair share of second-hand puffs.*"

She burst out laughing.

"*Interesting read*" I added.

"*Yeah, I am more than halfway now.*" She replied.

"*You have read this?*" She asked as she patted the ash off the cigarette.

"*Yeah, I have.*"

"*Honestly, please don't judge but this is the only Paulo Coelho that I have actually finished reading.*" I added with my brows raised and a soft giggle.

"*Wow, I can see your taste*" She said with a mischievous grin.

"*Can't be a coincidence, the only book you read of him is known for having the most intimate scenes.*" She added.

I broke into a laughter.

"*Alright, you got me*" I said lifting my hands up in a playful surrender.

"*So, what are you doing here?*" She asked as she flicked the cigarette butt into the corner.

"*Well, I am trying to write a piece myself but I am having a writer's block*" I replied.

"*And… trust me, it's not a sex story.*"

She laughed out loud. "*Can't trust you boy, I already have a picture painted of you now.*"

"*Well, let me put forward an empty canvas, so you can paint a new one.*"

"*I am Kshitij*" I put my hand forward, we shook hands.

"I am aspiring to be a writer and currently working on a contemporary fiction."

"I am a techie by profession by the way, but I took a big leap of faith, and I am currently on a sabbtical, trying to complete my book." I took a long breath after giving her a gist of my present.

"Nice to meet you Kshitij, I am Kanika."

"Well, your story seems interesting, unlike mine." She added.

"I work in corporate, have a daughter, sometimes I read. Honestly, I have a trunk full of shopping bags, as I was shopping for my daughter's college. Well, she made a long list, what can I say?"

"She will be moving soon to college hostel"

"That's me."

"Wow" I blurted. I knew she was older, but her daughter joining a college was not something that I was expecting.

"I am going to add a big cliche that I am sure you must have heard numerous times, but, damn, you look great, and I definitely was not expecting for your daughter to be in college"

I added, as I was honestly surprised, or maybe impressed, even I wasn't sure what it was.

"It's always good to hear this!" She laughed.

"Would you like to join me for a cup of coffee, and maybe help me with my first draft." I asked with a hint of nervousness. I was not sure if it was because of the age difference, or simply the fact that we'd only met fifteen minutes ago, but something made me hesitate.

"Yeah sure, although I had my dose of caffeine for today, I will rather get something to eat."

We walked to my table, and we sat down together.

She skimmed through my draft, suggested a few changes, and we ended up discussing possible storylines. We sat there chatting, and before we could realise it was already dark, time just flew by.

"It's getting late, I should leave." She said, glancing at the time.

"Yeah, sure," I replied, closing my laptop. I had to head home too.

We both walked out of the cafe to the car parking.

"That's mine." she pointed to her car.

We stopped walking. A moment of silence lingered in the air and something felt incomplete. We had a great time together and now it was about to be over.

"Hey, I had a good time today. Do you mind sharing contacts, I would love to hang out again."

"Of course, only if it's not an issue. I understand you are married, your husband obviously wouldn't like it."

I blurted out, as I wasn't really sure if that was appropriate. But I really liked her company, and didn't want to let go without saying anything.

She took a pause, smiled.

"I am separated." She replied.

It shook me.

I looked at her eyes, behind the smile and all the chatter, there was gloominess. It looked empty, somehow. I didn't know what to say.

"Yeah, it was nice." She added, with a bleak smile on her face.

"I am sorry, and I didn't mean to." I somehow managed to utter something as I had no idea how to respond to it.

"Don't worry, I am happy." She replied, caressing my arm.

"I guess, I am." She added.

I could see her battling to put her emotions in words.

After a long pause, I said.

"I definitely know less than you in terms of life experiences, but I would say one thing…"

"When we lose someone, we often lose the idea of happiness along with it. Every smile that we carve on our face, every thought that makes us happy, feels wrong."

"We have an absurd idea of surrounding ourselves with loneliness and bitterness, but I have understood it over time that getting our life back is not cheating. Living again, enjoying moments again is not wrong. Life is a cycle, moments don't define us until we let it."

"I lost my mum, it's been two years now. I wasn't there when she took her last breath."

"So, I know how it feels when you start to smile again, enjoy the moments again."

"I know it's very different for us, but you can't give up living."

I said, as I leaned against her car's door.

She held my hand, crossing her fingers through mine. We had the whole street in front of us, but we were looking at "nothing", lost in our thoughts, completely oblivious to the surrounding.

KANIKA

"Hey, done with the packing?" I saw the notification, it was a text from Kshitij.

It's been almost a month now since we met. We have been texting quite frequently and sometimes we spoke on the phone as well.

"Yeah, I am done. Well, it was quite a task. :D :D" I typed, but locked the phone instantly as I heard the door thud open.

"Mum, can you please complete the web check-in, the window is open now." Anya barged into the room, picked up her backpack, and left the room immediately.

"Sure!" I replied, although I knew she wasn't really waiting for an answer. Ma'am gave me a command and left the room.

"Hey, where are you?" The phone vibrated again.

"Heyy.. sorry Anya was here." I replied, and sent the last typed message, which was still sitting there unsent.

"No issues!"

"Well, the day has almost arrived, she will be off to college soon. How are you feeling, it must be a big change." I read the message again. It hit me all of a sudden. I have

been too busy lately to realise that a big part of me is going away.

Listening to her tantrums, laughing at her silly jokes, engaging in her gossip from school and her teenage problems, it's all going to fade away now. It's a new phase for her, she will be busy with new people, new friends. I will not be a part of those conversations anymore.

All these thoughts started to float around, and I was just lost amid.

"I know it's going to be tough, but you're not alone. I'm here for you." :)"

There was another text.

"I know :)"

"I am just happy that she got a great college, and things are finally falling in place for her. She has worked really hard for it" I typed, staring at the screen, my mind still clouded by the thought of her leaving. I guess I was afraid to accept that I was going to be lonely again.

Well, I've been lonely for a long time, but this time it felt like it was going to be worse. After my separation from my husband, she was always on my side, always looking out for me. Even though she was too young to understand everything, she still stood by me, talking to me every night, checking on me, making sure I was okay.

Although I talked to her about most of the things, I was still bottled up with years of struggle and loneliness. There were several nights when I cried myself to sleep. All of this stayed buried deep inside my heart and I never let it surface. I knew I had to be a strong woman, a strong mother. I had to take care of her.

Amid all these I never really could find joy for myself. I refrained myself from joy and every piece of happiness that came to me. Somewhere, something always pulled me back. Being a single mother wasn't easy. Life changed in a lot of ways that I couldn't imagine. But at the end of the day, what mattered the most was that she was happy.

My phone started ringing, it was him on a video call.

"Hey, what happened?" He asked. I could see his gloomy eyes looking at mine, as if he knew almost everything that was running through my mind.

"Nothing…"

"Nothing really…!" I replied feebly, trying to hold my tears. I knew I was going to break down any minute.

He kept looking at me silently. No words were exchanged, we both just looked at each other. I heard a song playing in the background, he increased the volume. We were still looking into each other's eyes. My heart felt lighter, as if it poured out everything to him, even though I didn't say a word.

I could see him smile, as if he knew exactly how I was feeling. I smiled back, as a wave of relief surrounded me.

"Thanks for being there!" I whispered.

"I am always there for you!" He mumbled, leaning closer to the camera.

It's been just a month since I met him, yet somehow it feels longer. I've never really been able to open up to anyone, but with him it was different. I somehow opened all my secret doors to him. I don't know whether it was him being a good listener, or me who needed to let things out, but somehow it happened. And just like that, we grew closer.

It felt like he understood me, a lot better. Of course I liked it, but at times it felt wrong. Though he never asked my age I knew that he was quite younger than me. I often judge myself for opening up to him, getting closer to him, as I know we have no future ahead, it's meaningless. Although lately I have found myself smiling often, admiring myself in the mirror, replaying every compliment he gave me, loving myself a little more. So, yeah, even though it was wrong, it felt right.

KSHITIJ

"Hi papa, you haven't eaten yet, sorry I got late today" I said as I walked inside the house using the spare key I had.

"I was waiting for you, like always." He chuckled.

We both shared a laugh and walked to the kitchen. I served dinner while he helped.

"How was the day? Did you make any progress on the story?" He asked.

"Yeah dad, slightly. I wasn't able to decide the storyline earlier, but now I do." I replied collecting my thoughts.

Well, losing my mom, and now meeting Kanika and hearing her story made me realise how fragile time can be, and how it can mould your life in a totally unexpected way.

All the plans, ambitions and goals that people look onto their whole lives can shatter in a moment and everything gets washed away with the weight of a single wave.

I have often clung to the promises of a better tomorrow and never really lived in the present fully, but lately I realised a content life is all about choosing what you like, going for it, and not looking back. For me, I wouldn't want regrets years from now, regretting lost time.

It's been a few months since dad moved in with me, and life has felt different ever since. Living with a single parent at this stage of my life comes with its own adjustments, balancing my ambitions, my career, my space, and the quiet need for companionship at home. It's just a strange in-between phase, where you're still figuring things out while also trying to take care of someone you love.

It's not that I can't go out or live my life the way I used to, it's just that I don't want him sitting alone at home waiting for me to return. He's lonely now, and losing a partner does something to a person that time can't easily heal. I don't want him to feel that ache every single day. With work taking up most of my hours, I hardly get the time to sit with him and have a real conversation.

These days, since I have been off work, I try to spend as much time as I can with him. Either planning dinners or trips, I don't give it a second thought anymore. With my mother gone and so many plans left undone, I realised there is never a perfect time for something. The moment matters, and the memories we create together, after all, this is what stays with us forever.

Sometimes the wait never ends, it just drifts into forever.

"Hey! Surprisingly I have quite a lot to say, but don't really know how to."

"It was lovely meeting you today, I had a great time. I would love to get to know you better, well, of course only if you feel the same way."

And thank you for, ummm… all the passive puffs today, hope I don't get addicted :D :D"

I edited the message quite a few times and sent this one finally.

It was almost 11 at night, and I still hadn't received a reply. Somewhere deep down, I was anxious, trying hard not to delete the message. I felt nervous, maybe even a little ashamed, wondering if I had overthought it, maybe it had been nothing more than a casual meeting.

I kept checking the phone but finally decided to keep it away.

Then I saw her typing….

"Hey! I am sorry, I was busy going through all the shopping with Anya."

"And yeah, likewise, it was nice talking to you."

She sent.

I saw she reacted with red heart emoji on my message, and so I did the same with her text.

"Haha, oh no ;) ;) … don't tell me you're already addicted! You better be careful, it's bad for your health."

I read her message and laughed .

"HAHAHA, I will be careful, no promises though ;) :D"

I replied.

We chatted until 3 in the morning talking about her life, her work and Anya. She asked me about my dad and my family.

With hundreds of messages, a roller coaster of emotions, and more emojis than I could count, it felt like we were sharing pieces of ourselves with each other.

"Hey, how was the trip?"

My phone beeped, it was Kanika's text.

"*It was good. I will ping you in a bit. I came to a theatre to watch a movie with dad*" I replied.

My dad, being retired, staying in a city where he didn't know many people, I often tried to find something for him to do. I created a whole playlist of old movies on OTT platforms so that he could watch them.

And just like always, I played the movie for him and went back to my desk for work, since the day had been quite hectic. Later, when I walked in to check on him, the TV was off and he was just lying on the couch. I asked him why he turned off the TV as it was one of his favourite movies, and he smiled and said "*You were not here, and I didn't feel like watching alone.*"

That moment stayed with me. It made me realise that you can't buy happiness for the people you love, you show it by giving your time, presence, and the small efforts that you put in everyday.

A new family movie had released recently, so I decided to take him out to watch it together. This time with no work calls, no rushing back to my laptop.

We sat through the whole film side by side, shared laughs, popcorns and talked about scenes. Afterward, we grabbed dinner and talked a little more than usual on the drive back home. It wasn't anything extravagant, but it felt warm.

It was a simple yet a beautiful evening.

"Hey! Just came back home"

I texted as I asked Alexa to turn off the lights.

"And yeah, the trip was really nice. I planned it around his choices and preferences. I specifically booked the hotel right next to the Ashram which he wanted to visit. We attended meditation sessions, yoga classes, and the aarti. He loved it, and honestly, I did too."

I added further telling her about how the trip went. We got back from the trip yesterday after spending a few quiet days in Rishikesh and Haridwar.

My phone beeped again, it was her.

"You know, I really love this about you, the way you take him on trips, to movies, making sure he never feels alone. It shows how deeply you care. Not everyone has that kind of a heart. You're such a wonderful son. <3"

"Nowhere close yaar, just doing the least I can." I replied.

"Just trying…!" I added.

"The moving day is getting closer, how are you holding up?" I asked.

It was just a week until Anya moves to her hostel.

"She is happy, so am I." She replied.

"VC?" I asked.

"Yeah, two mins?" She replied.

We ended up video calling and talking for another two hours. It had been a little over a month since we first got to know each other, and we gradually became a part of each other's lives. In the last few days something had changed, our conversations felt warmer, our silences felt understood.

From sharing memes to exchanging pictures, from light-hearted jokes to late-night confessions, we opened up in ways neither of us had expected. Even the unspoken thoughts found their way across the screen. Somewhere in those moments, those tears, those stories, those little pieces of ourselves, we grew into something we couldn't name, but we both knew it was special. Something we needed, and maybe, deep down, something we both wanted.

WHEN THEY MET

"Hey, How are you doing?" Kanika saw the text. She locked the phone and kept it away.

She lay on the bed as the curtains swayed softly in the evening wind. With the sun setting, the room slowly slipped into darkness.

She unlocked her phone again and glanced at the time, with four consecutive hours of sleep, she was still tired. She checked for any missed calls or messages from Anya, there were none. Her eyes lingered on the screen a little longer hoping to see Anya's name light up, but it wasn't there

Kanika just got back today after dropping Anya at her college. She stayed there for three days to get her settled in. She saw Anya making new friends, slowly settling into her new phase of life.

As the city enveloped in darkness, while the high rise buildings glazed with brimming lights, she sat there looking out of the window, realising how lonely it had become for her. With so many places to go, and so many people to be with, she had nothing, emptiness had her engulfed.

With the lights still off, the room felt heavy and dim. The wind brushed against the curtains every now and then, and all she could do was keep her eyes open and let reality hit her, bit by bit, one truth after another, until it finally sank in that it was just her now.

She brewed a cup of coffee and sat in a corner of the room. Notifications kept popping on her phone, there were multiple messages from Kshitij along with a few missed calls.

With every sip, she went through the messages, staring at the screen, lost in her thoughts. She wanted to answer his calls, she wanted to reply to all of his texts, and to listen to his voice and to tell him everything about the trip and how she was feeling, but she didn't have enough courage to tap on the keys on her phone.

She was alone, vulnerable, and a little broken. Every wall of the room, every corner of the apartment, felt unbearably dreary.

She wanted him, desperately, achingly, but she knew that if he was here, she wouldn't be able to hold herself together. Everything she had curbed till now would break free, and there would be no going back from there.

Night had already settled in, yet she still couldn't pull herself back into her routine. She remained curled up in the corner, staring at her phone, rereading the texts from Kshitij.

She was fighting her thoughts, every single one of them, replaying everything in her mind over and over again. But there was no escaping the truth; if he had been beside her right now, she would have melted, like an ice on the fire.

"Hey Kshitij!"

"Sorry, I dozed. I was tired after all the travelling."

She replied acting as composed as she could.

She waited for a few minutes, but there was no reply. She looked at chat wondering if he was upset that she ignored him the entire day.

The very next moment her phone rang. It was him.

"Hey, I am at the gate of your building, can you let me in?"

"Yeah, sure" She said, still confused and a little stunned. He was already here, right at the gate?

"*Hey!*" He said, as she opened the door. He was standing there holding a bottle of wine and some flowers.

"Hey!"

"Hi" She uttered again after a pause, still surprised.

He stood there looking at her, her damp eyes, wrinkled shirt, smudged mascara. Before she could tell him anything, her eyes uttered it all.

"You will be fine, don't worry!" He said quietly, looking at the dark room behind her.

"I didn't mean to intrude, I just thought maybe you needed a company, so got a drink."

He paused, looking at her, struggling to understand her expression.

"Don't worry, I will leave if you want." He added nervously as she was still standing at the door, no words said, no gesture, just looking at him.

"Heyyyy! I am really sorry. C'mon, you are not at all intruding. Come in" She blurted, almost as if she had just snapped out of a dream.

They walked in, Kshitij took to the couch while Kanika turned on the lights of the apartment. The darkness dissolved with every clicks of the switches. He looked at her, her untied hair dangling with each step she took, her skin glowing in the golden warm light.

She came and sat on the couch opposite him. There was silence, a long one.

Kshitij sat there, nervously, looking around every inch of the walls that stood in front of him. His eyes hovered over hers, and then back to some awkward corner.

"I will get some glasses!" Kanika got up and walked to the kitchen. She knew both of them were too nervous to even exchange words sober.

"Thanks for the bottle by the way, you got me my favourite wine." She said placing the glasses in front of him. She took the seat next to him, on the same couch this time.

"I knew you needed one today." He said with a bleak smile.

The silence between them echoed louder than words. She poured the drinks, and their glasses touched, a soft clink cutting through the tension as they took the first sip.

"I know why you were distant the whole day, and I totally understand. I just wanted to be here with you."

"That's all." He said, breaking the long streak of silence.

"I know." She replied with a nod.

She paused, and poured another one for both of them.

This time she went ahead and gulped the whole glass of wine in one go.

"And I wanted to call you quite a few times but I was trying really hard not to." She added, looking at the wall, as if she was talking to herself. It sounded more like a confession from her, she had to gather a lot of courage just to say it to him.

"You are not alone, you should know that." Kshitij murmured, looking into her eyes as he leaned further and placed his hands on hers.

"I know!" She whispered, her voice trembling.

"And thanks!" she curled her fingers around his, holding him tighter.

"You know it's been seven years since I have been separated, and I never really had a day for myself. I was always looking out for Anya. It was a big change for her and I always tried my best to never let her feel the absence of a parent."

"Since then, I don't think I've had a single day that truly felt like mine. Somewhere along the way, I lost myself trying to hold everything else together."

"I never went on a date, never did something that I enjoyed, never had time just to myself. It felt like I stopped living for me altogether."

"Yeah, I didn't message you or call since I came back. I didn't want to burden you with this. I am a mess, and we have never talked about it directly but it's going to be a mess for you, being here, being with me, being with someone much older than you."

"You are a great guy, and of course I like your company, but this isn't going to work for either of us."

She poured everything out, everything she had buried in her heart.

"You don't need to explain this to me. I am not a teen. I know what I want, and I know what I am walking into."

"And honestly I don't care about anything else, I know we have the age gap, and our lives are on different paths, but I like being with you, talking to you."

"Yeah, I like you."

"Here, I said it."

Kshitij said, leaning towards her. Her eyes melted, a tear drop dropped down her eyes.

She was not ready to let go of him this time, to dismiss the love that walked toward her with open arms. She sat there speechless, reframing sentences again and again in her mind but unable to utter a word.

"You don't have to say that you like me too, it doesn't matter. I just had to tell you how I felt."

"I don't want to carry regrets in my life Kanika. I don't want to sit wondering several years later whether I should have told you when the time was right and expressed what I had in my heart."

"I don't care what five years later looks like for us, or maybe even a year. We are here right now, let's live in the present."

"Don't you think you finally deserve something for yourself."

His every word slammed into her ears. She wanted to shriek out loud and tell him "Yes", that she wanted him, but she sat still as silence had her engulfed.

They both knew they wanted each other, but it was always the consequences, the future, that made them rethink their choices. But tonight it changed, all the feelings they had for each other, they were finally ready to let it out.

He leaned and held her by her arms. She was closer than ever, he could hear her heart thumping, her hair brushing against his shoulders, her eyelids fluttering in front of his. The fragrance of her body enveloped him as he pulled her closer and put his lips over hers, gently.

With her eyes closed, her lips embraced his and they smooched. Their tongue swirled around quenching each other's thirst as if they had been starved for decades.

They took a pause, looking into each other's eyes. He gently pushed her hair to the side while gazing at her bare skin. He let his lips run wet, smudging all over her neck. He could hear her soft moans which grew further as his lips went deeper down her chest.

He unbuttoned her shirt one by one, while his lips smeared the glister all over her cleavage. He dropped her shirt on the floor.

Kanika sat on his lap, with her legs wrapped around his waist, her hair dangling all over, enveloping his face. She leaned forward and took his tee out.

She took a cigarette from the pack and lit it.

"You really should stay away from smokers" Kanika laughed as she took a puff. She exhaled slowly over his mouth.

As she took another puff, Kshitij tangled her hair around his wrist and pulled her closer, slowly, and smooched her. She let go off the smoke inside him slowly. Beneath the wisp of smoke hovering over them, the clothes slimmed down and their passion peaked.

He slowly slid his hand down, she gasped. He touched her, down there, feeling the wetness inside, while she moaned with her lips running over his shoulders. With one hand hovering inside her knickers and another unhooking her bra, he dropped them on the floor. His lips fondled her busts, while she swayed on top of him, her nails piercing his skin, leaving marks of pleasure. The night grew longer and so did their expression of love.

"Get ready, I will take you somewhere." Kshitij said, as he buttoned his shirt.

"Where?" Kanika asked curiously, since it was already midnight.

"You will know on the way, c'mon, get dressed" He said handing over her clothes. He picked up his car keys while Kanika got dressed.

"Seriously, where are we going?" She asked again as they cruised along the empty roads of the city.

"You will get to know." He replied and kept driving.

"Ohh, I figured" She exclaimed as she looked at the beautiful sight. Kanika spotted the shore from afar and she knew exactly where they were heading to.

Kshitij parked the car by the roadside and they walked towards Marine drive.

The view was mesmerising, waves crashing against the rocks on one side, and towering high-rises shimmering under the moonlight on the other.

"Here you go" Kshitij said, as he handed Kanika her cup of tea.

They sat there sipping tea, with the cold winds gushing and waves splashing them every once in a while.

Kanika heard her phone ring, it was Anya video calling her. She looked at Kshitij, unsure if she should pick up the call, wondering what to tell her and how to explain who she was with.

He tapped on her shoulder and asked her to go ahead and pick it up.

She hesitated for a moment, but picked it up before it was about to disconnect.

"Hey Mom" Anya said.

"Wow, where are you?" She asked surprisingly as she understood that Kanika wasn't at home.

"Hey Anya, how are you?" Kanika replied ignoring her question.

"I am good mum, everything's well. Was about to go to sleep, so thought of calling you." Anya said, while Kanika

was trying to adjust her camera so that Anya doesn't get to see Kshitij.

The very next moment, the tea vendor walked to them and said *"Brother, I have got the change."*

Kanika was taken aback by this, she didn't know what to say. Anya understood that she was with some guy.

"Maa, have a good night! And don't worry, I am happy for you!" Anya said with a smile as she understood her discomfort.

Kanika responded with a smile. She had never imagined telling Anya about any other man, but she was happy, and proud that she understood her, and wanted to see her happy and live her life.

A CASUAL NIGHT

DEEPTI

I was about to reach Mumbai in the next two hours. It was my first ever solo trip. I was born and brought up in Lucknow, and had completed my college there and then got a job in the same city. So, I never really got to leave the city and live away from my family, on my own. I was really desperate to go out and settle in a different city, start a new life, and meet new people. I was always shadowed by someone from the family almost everywhere. I never realised that over time, I started developing grievances for the fact that I wasn't allowed to be independent. At my age when other friends were moving to different cities, going abroad, partying, clubbing, going on road trips and all this time I just got to stay at home and go one some family trips, rarely.

I was going to Mumbai to visit my friend. It was a one-week trip and I really needed an escape. My parents had already started planning for my marriage and it was suffocating for me, being at home listening to all the discussions about my marriage, the planning, and almost everything.

I reached there by 5:00 p.m. The weather was pleasant. I took a cab to my friend's apartment. It was almost an hour's ride.

I reached the place. It was a huge society with numerous residential buildings. All around thirty storeys. Neha was there to pick me up at the gate.

She lived with one of her other friends in a 2 BHK apartment. I settled in her room while she finished up some of her office work on her laptop.

"*Okay Deepti, get ready. Today we are going to a party.*" She said as she shut the flap of her laptop.

"*Now?*" I looked at her, still surprised. I couldn't even get enough rest.

"*Yeah, it's Friday night.*"

"*You have got to see the parties here.*" She continued as she unzipped my bag.

She made me try a few one-piece dresses. I didn't have many, but I got hooked to one red dress. She pulled one black dress for herself. She looked amazing. If I was a guy, I knew I would be hitting on her.

We reached the place just twenty mins before the happy hour starts. We were three of us, me, Neha and her flatmate, Ananya. While we were waiting in the queue to get stamped, a guy approached me.

"*Hey, sorry to bother. Actually, we are three guys and they aren't allowing stag entry. Could you guys please help us out?*" He said. Neha was just behind me, listening all of this.

We turned out around to see the other guys, there were two others standing in a corner. They smiled softly.

I just turned around to check with Neha and everyone else, but before I could say anything, she already blurted out "*Sure, you can join us.*"

"*They are cute,*" Neha said with a chuckle and winked as the guy walked back to his friends.

I just looked at her blandly, it was all very new to me and I had no idea if it was okay.

They all joined us the next moment. We all walked together pretending to be couples, got stamped, and walked inside.

We parted as we entered the place. The three of us got a table near the dance floor, which seemed to be the perfect spot, standing quite close to the bar.

I saw both of them jumping straight to the bar menu, they ordered multiple shots and drinks as the happy hour was right about to end and in just a few minutes our table had all sort of drinks spread across.

We sat there sipping our drinks while crunching the fries and the pizza. It was almost an hour since we were there and I was already three drinks down. Well, we were going slow, especially me, because I have had drinks just a few countable times in my life and I knew I wouldn't be able to handle a lot.

"*C'mon, let's hit the dance floor.*" Neha stood up as she finished her drink in a go.

We all walked to the dance floor; it was moderately crowded. The DJ started some Punjabi music and the crowd wooed. We danced along with the music, slipping into the rhythm, letting the beats surge through us until the rest of the room faded away. The next moment, I noticed the guys standing at the side of the dance floor, the same ones we had entered the club with.

"*You want a drink?*" One of the guys approached and asked Neha, holding a glass of whiskey.

"*No, I am kind of done. Thanks!*" She replied.

"*Well, you guys helped us. This is the least I can do.*" He said with a smile.

"*Uhh, well...*" Neha was just wondering how to respond while we were looking at them.

"*C'mon, one drink. There's no harm,*" he said with a chuckle, nudging the glass toward her. She took a sip, then another, and before she could finish it, he gently took the glass from her hand and downed the rest in one swift go.

"*Shall we?*" he asked, taking her hand as he set the glass down on a corner table.

The two of them slipped back onto the dance floor, leaving us watching from where we stood. A little later, the other guys drifted over and joined us, and soon we were all moving together to the music.

By the time the night wore on, our legs were tired and the energy had mellowed. We settled around a table, and the guys joined us there.

It was already late and we were planning to leave . We sat there waiting for Neha to come back from the restroom so that we could leave.

Looking around the table I stumbled upon Neha, and saw her talking to the guy in one corner. He was Shrey, the same guy with whom she was dancing. They seemed to get along nicely.

Neha walked to me and asked "*Hey, he is asking me out tonight. I am thinking I should bring him to our place rather than going to his.*"

"*Will that be okay? I am sorry I know should not bail out like this.*" She continued as Ananya joined our conversation.

"*That's okay Neha, she will stay with me tonight. We are already tired, so we just need to sleep.*" She said. "*Not you of course.*" She added with a wink. We laughed.

I was kind of surprised about the fact that he was coming over as she just met her like a few hours back. Ananya looked at me and smiled, we walked to the cab that had just arrived.

We reached home, Neha and Shrey were with us in the drawing room and then later they went into her bedroom and locked it from inside.

I sat there with Ananya on the couch. It was just us, who barely knew each other and had met for the first time. We hovered through the topics of our family, work, about Neha and everything else that we could talk about.

It was already midnight and we were starving, After scrolling through food delivery apps for about fifteen minutes, we finally decided to go with Maggi.

"*So, what's your plan for the next few days?*" She asked while I served the Maggi.

"*Nothing much, haven't planned yet. I might visit a few places. I have made the whole list btw, I said pointing to my phone.*" I replied.

I showed her the list of the places that I made and the cafes that I had planned to visit. She pointed out the overhyped ones, suggested me quite a few food joints and some places to definitely visit.

We were just sitting there when we heard a thud from inside Neha's bedroom. It appeared that something fell, or someone. The next moment we heard giggling. We just looked at each other and smiled. We both knew something was going on there.

As we gulped down the last bits from the Maggi bowl, we heard something again. I was dumbstruck. I could hear her moans, clearly. I was too embarrassed to even look at Ananya, I just sat there holding the bowl in my hand with my eyes glued on the floor.

Ananya sensed my discomfort and took me to her room.

"*I know this is all new to you, and I know how it really feels.*" She looked at me as she said.

"*Well, don't know if it's wrong or right, but casual sex is really common these days.*" She added.

I nodded. I just didn't know how to respond.

"*I was in a marriage, I tried my best to be a good wife , but it didn't really get me anything.*"

I looked at her. I had no idea that she was married. She looked young, and I never saw her wearing any sindoor.

"I got divorced two years back. I married at a young age, tried to give up everything for the marriage to hold onto it but it didn't take me anywhere. I left my job, lived with in-laws, had almost no social life, but over the time I realised that is not how I was supposed to be."

"Well, maybe I look young, but I am 32. One complete year I spent in remorse and cursing myself that I couldn't hold onto a marriage, but I tried really hard. I know, somewhere even my family blames me for not doing enough to keep the marriage."

"Yeah, it was ugly, trust me."

"But in the end, I realised it was me who really cares about myself and nobody else, and I am the only one responsible for my own life. So, I took some hard decisions and here I am, earning good, living a life I wanted, happy. I am certainly much happier than I was in that marriage."

"Sometimes even I indulge in a causal fling, and maybe that's because I am done with the serious ones."

"You know it's all about the complications that follow along when you start aligning two people together, to be with each other, and I really didn't want that anymore in my life."

"I am not saying if it's right or wrong, but what I know is sometimes it's okay to live out for yourself. At least no one's getting hurt here."

"You know it's kind of simple, not knowing, no promises, we get what we want and then it's over. There are no complications, expectations, and all."

I just sat there listening to her, trying to construe whatever she just said. She was somewhere right, maybe.

Aarav

"*Sir, you have a meeting in an hour. We need to leave in 10 mins.*" Mira said as she picked up the files from the desk and my iPad.

"*Okay, I will be ready.*" I replied.

Mira brought me another blazer from the wardrobe on the backside of my office. "*I have got it dry cleaned and here is your juice sir.*" She kept the glass on the table.

"*Sir, it will be the BMW today?*" Mira asked as she helped me with the blazer.

"*No, get the Maybach.*" I replied as I sipped down the juice in one go.

Mira called my chauffeur and informed him to get the car. In no time we were in the elevator and then inside my car headed for the meeting. Mira sat beside me while I was looking through the charts on my laptop. Mira, being my assistant had a lot of things to handle for me which of course made my life somewhat easier.

The meeting was really important for me and the company, so I had to put a lot of effort into it. This was a big client and this was supposed to be the final discussion today to seal the deal.

The meeting lasted for almost one hour. It certainly was good as I knew I didn't leave any stone unturned to convince the client. The deal was sealed. It was one of the biggest clients for us now.

"*Aarav, Congratulations! I am glad you got the client. I know you worked really hard for it.*" Mira said as she handed me a small wrapped gift.

"*We did it Mira, not me.*"

"*What is this Mira?*" I added I was surprised as she offered me the gift.

"*Please accept it! I just want you to have it.*" Mira said as she handed me the gift.

"*Please!*" She added again.

I took the gift and unwrapped it as she asked me to. It was Parker Premier's exclusive edition pen. It was elegant.

"*Mira, thanks a lot, but you didn't have to do this.*" I looked at her.

She just smiled and cupped my hand with hers. "*This is the least I can do.*"

I smiled back and thanked her. Yes, this deal meant a lot for us and undoubtedly Mira had always been on my side, helping me out at every footstep.

"*Mira, I will have a party tonight at my home and you have to come.*" I said.

"*Yes sir, I will.*" Mira nodded.

"*We are not in office yet, no need for sir.*" I added with a smile as the car entered the parking of the office building.

It was eight in the evening. The party was about to start in some time. I put on my best-tailored suite and was waiting for the guests to join in sometime.

While I waited, I took a glass of whiskey and walked to the porch. I stood there sipping down the scotch, glancing out of the penthouse apartment. It felt like I was gathering everything that I had ever dreamt of in bits and pieces. It had been almost ten years since I came to Mumbai for the first time in search of a job, and here I was after all the struggle and hustle. I built my company from scratch and expanded it to what it is today. Maybe I was running too fast that I couldn't even and turn back and see what I was leaving behind. I was in a relationship a long time back but since the breakup, I never looked back. I just had to achieve everything that I had always wanted.

Today, it feels like I have gotten along so far in this race and have achieved almost everything that I had ever wanted, but sometimes at the end of the day, it does feel lonely. I often think that it would have been good to have someone by my side, along the beautiful journey.

I stood there on the porch, looking at the city. It looked beautiful in the evening, enveloped by darkness while everyone was rushing down the lanes fighting for their goals and chasing the dreams.

"*Hey Mira, glad you came.*" I greeted her as I saw her coming inside the apartment. A few of the guests had already arrived.

People were enjoying the soft music while sipping down the blended scotch and imported wines. I was there, greeting them, thanking them, and then moving on. It felt incomplete even after being surrounded by so many people. I entertained them with all the exotic cuisines and drinks and then grabbed a glass and went again to the porch. I sat there watching through the glass wall, inhaling the music while sipping down the whiskey. Even after having everything that I had ever wanted, I felt incomplete.

"*Hi, Aarav! I hope I am not disturbing you.*" I turned around. It was Mira.

"*No, of course not. C'mon!*" I said.

She stood beside me leaning on the glass wall.

"*Should I pour you one?*" I asked as I signalled an attendant to bring one.

"*Yeah, sure.*" She nodded.

We stood there talking about the company, growth, clients, and just everything else, while avoiding the topics we really wanted to discuss, about our personal lives.

We could hear the music playing from behind and some noise of blabbering people, fading away with every drink that ran through our throat. It was a breezy evening with cold wind flowing around.

"*What is that you are thinking?*" She asked as she moved closer to me, our hands brushed. I could feel her heartbeat racing. She sipped another drink down.

I comforted myself as I adjusted my hands away slightly, hers were still close to mine.

"*I don't know. It's just sometimes I feel that I have everything that I had ever dreamt of but still, it feels incomplete.*"

"*I just had been working really hard for this day, and now over the time, it looks like I have lost myself somewhere.*" I completed as I took another sip of the scotch.

"*I have worked with you for three years now, I know how much you have put in your time and effort for everything you have now.*" Mira said.

I felt a hand over my shoulders. It was hers. "*Sometimes you need to take the back seat and think of something else, something that your heart wants.*"

"*Maybe now is the time for you to think of something else, take a break, and look forward to your life.*" Mira said, as she came closer and held my hand, caressing it over the metal ceiling of the glass wall.

I felt the warmth of her hand, against the cold metal. I just wanted to live in the moment, but I wasn't sure if that was right. She was my co-worker. Perhaps, it was the scotch, but it felt good, it felt lively.

"*Hey Aarav, it's been a while.*" A voice interrupted. I turned back. I was surprised to see her here.

"*Hey Shruti, great seeing you again.*" I responded. The next moment she came and hugged me.

"*It's a surprise to see you. I thought you wouldn't be coming.*" I uttered in shock.

"*Well, I came. C'mon, let's join the party.*" Shruti held my hand and pulled me inside the apartment. I turned around to see Mira standing there watching us. Before I could react or say anything everyone else surrounded us for the party.

We celebrated for a while, pouring down drinks. Shruti was sitting beside me telling me about herself, and how life has been since the last time we met. Shruti is a journalist so we met a few times for work and meetings. She was more like a friend now, though we weren't in regular contact.

We sat on the couch while Shruti was sipping wine and I was pouring down the scotch. Mira was in another corner sitting by herself. I got completely engrossed with Shruti that I couldn't even get to talk to her again.

It was almost midnight when most of the people were totally drunk. They started leaving and in no time the place was almost empty.

"*Aarav, I should leave now.*" Mira said as she walked past the door. I looked at her, I felt she was upset.

"*Hey Mira, it was nice talking to you.*" I said as she was waiting for the elevator.

"*Thanks!*" She smiled bluntly.

"*Mira, take my car. The chauffeur will drop you at your place.*"

"*Thanks, Aarav, but I will take a cab.*" She said.

The elevator was there. She walked in, I followed her. I looked at her, she was frowning.

I walked her to my Merc, the chauffeur was waiting for us.

I held her hand as she walked in and took the seat.

"*Thank you!*" She said.

I smiled looking at her. Until then, I hadn't realised how beautiful she was looking in her purple dress with dark lipstick. The lights of the cabin were reflecting her skin tone perfectly in the dark.

"*Text me once you reach.*" I waved and then she left.

I went back to my apartment, almost everybody left by then. Only Shruti was there, she was sitting on the couch.

"*Hey Mr, finally you are free.*" She giggled as she handed me a glass of whiskey.

I sat by her side as I took a sip from the glass. The whole apartment was empty now. After we poured a few drinks, she held my hand and walked into my bedroom.

I was almost drunk, as I could feel slight dizziness. I followed her. She changed the tracks slowly and I dimmed the lights with the voice command. I wasn't sure what was really happening, I was just following her lead.

The next moment she pulled me behind the door and leaned further. Before I could think of anything, she just came closer. I stood there petrified, unaware of what to think. My mind was clouded and so were my senses, and the very next moment I felt her lips on mine. I wasn't sure what it was, but I reciprocated.

I could feel the warmth of her body over mine. Her lips brushed mine while her fingers were running over my bare chest as she unbuttoned my shirt.

I just curled my tongue along hers and kissed her, holding her tight. She put off my shirt and then started kissing me on the shoulders, and then the neck. I felt my body trembling with every touch of her lips over my skin. I felt her hand running down on me and my heart was racing. The next moment I pulled down the zip of her dress and fondled her busts which were wrapped in her black brassiere. I kissed her over her neck and then her cleavage. I could almost hear her heart racing with every touch of mine.

The next moment she pulled me in the bed. There I was, lying, as she came on my top, throbbing herself on me. I just lied there biting my lips while she had the moments of pleasure. I came on top of her, smooched her till we were out of breath. I ran my lips over her bare skin as she breathed heavily. With her every breathe I fondled her and kissed her while she moaned gently. It was like the warmth in heaven where the whole world was melting. I went down gradually while she shivered, piercing her nails over my shoulders. I kissed her navel and run my lips around while she had her eyes closed and her lips dry and mumbling.

I took the ice cube from the glass and put it gently over her skin. She almost screamed as she felt the freezing cold over her skin. I wrapped the ice cube with my lips and moved it gently over her bare skin. She moaned while I went down and the ice melted slowly.

We wrapped ourselves in the darkness and made love for the rest of the night.

DEEPTI

It was yet another day in Mumbai. We spent almost the whole day exploring the city together. It was evening when we got back to our apartment.

"*Guys, I just received a call, Shantanu and his friends are having an in-house party. He has invited us as well. You guys wanna go?*" Neha asked looking at Ananya and me.

"*Ya, let's go. She will get to meet everyone. It will be your first in house party I guess, huh?*" Ananya asked smiling at me.

I nodded.

"*Well, you might get some fun as well, it often gets wild.*" Neha giggled and winked.

"*Okay let's do it.*" Ananya said.

"*They are our neighbours, they usually host parties like this and invite us, so don't worry they are friendly.*" Neha added.

After a while, we freshened up and left for their apartment. It was in the same society, just a few blocks away in another building.

"*Hey everyone.*" Shantanu opened the door for us.

We went inside, I introduced myself to everyone else. I seemed to be the only new person. I looked around. It was a big apartment with five guys living there as I later learned. We got seated on the couch, in the hall and then there were bean bags and mats spread across. I looked at one corner there was a guy doing something behind the table.

I was curious about why he there alone, so I walked over to see.

"*Hey*" He looked up. It was kind of weird, I felt as I am intruding someone's privacy.

"*Hie*" I replied.

"*Sorry to disturb, I was just curious what is it.*" I said as I looked at him, holding his office's visiting card with some greenish powder on it. I really wasn't sure what was it. It looked weird, some kind of herb. I had no clue.

He giggled. "*Well, this is the dessert for the party.*" He offered me a seat beside him.

"*This is weed, I need to crush the granules properly so as to make it perfect.*" I sat beside him and then he told me about the whole process about how he cleared the stuff, and then crushing the granules, separating them, and then rolling them in the OCB paper.

I was just laughing while listening to the whole process and the dedication with which he was doing it.

"*I know I know. I should have concentrated this much during my IIT entrance examinations.*" He said and we burst into laughter.

"*This is an art.*" He said with a giggle. We laughed together, he was funny and I kind of got comfortable around him. He was Gaurav, in case I forgot to tell you.

The party started, and after some time a few other people joined. There were almost 15 people at the party, dancing, telling stories, and of course some whining about their breakups and relationships.

There was a foldable table which was converted into a minibar. There were bottles of scotch, rum, and vodka kept on the table, and then there was a hookah pot kept on the other side. Three to four people always had the table surrounded, passing around the hookah tubes and inhaling while others were making drinks.

We started a game "Beer Pong", where the cups filled with beer were arranged in a pyramid shape on each side of the big dining table. We were divided into two teams and we had to throw a table tennis ball on the other side of the table. The rule was such that if the ball falls into one of the cups, someone from the team of that side has to pick up the cup and drink the beer in a go.

Honesty, it was totally fine in the beginning but later when there were just a few glasses left and people were just too drunk to have any more sips, it got fun. I could see some of them begging to their teammates to drink the rest from the cup.

It was almost 1 and most of us were drunk or stoned. I looked around, someone was lying with their face on the floor and legs on the couch, while other was lying adjoining two bean bags together.

My phone started vibrating, I checked it was one of my friends calling. I hurried and walked inside the room. There was too much noise in the hall.

I just pushed the door of the room and I was surprised. I just uttered sorry a few times and moved out. It was Ananya with one of the guys on her top, in just her bra.

I looked around most of the rooms were locked, there was one at the other end. I went and took the call and then joined back in the hall. I couldn't see Neha as well, which later Gaurav told me that she was in another room.

Well, it was just us and other couples locked up in other rooms. Almost everybody else left for their own apartments or were sleeping somewhere.

"*You wanna try this?*" Gaurav asked as he saw me sitting alone. He pulled out a joint stick towards me.

I giggled. "*Really? No, not this.*" I said. He sat beside me.

"*C'mon, it's a shortcut to heaven. Just make sure we have enough snacks in the kitchen.*" "*I guess we have.*" He added as he leaped towards the kitchen.

My phone beeped. It was a message from Ananya. "*Go, girl, have some fun. Gaurav should be available. Yeah, I saw you guys earlier. :P*" I read the message as I saw him smoking up the joint.

My phone beeped again. It was her again. "*Well, in case you do, there are some condoms, it's kept beneath the left most cushion of the couch. Yeah, that's a convenient place, you can try it there as well. :P :D everyone is too wasted to notice.*"

"*Here you go, whatever you need.*" Gaurav brought some chips, peanuts, and a few chicken wings.

"*Seriously?*" I looked at him as he lit the joint and handed it to me.

"*There's no harm.*" He smiled.

He told me to take the puff gradual and small and then release it slowly. I took the first one and puffed it out. It wasn't that harsh. He took the stick and took a puff and then gave it back to me.

We smoked up there while feasting on the chicken legs with some soft music playing in the background. We talked about all kinds of stuff, he told me about his road trips, his college journey, and then the job while I sat there listening to him. I didn't really have a lot to contribute, all I told him was about my job, my family, and my life over there.

The next moment I saw him lean, he was closer now. We were alone and the music was fainting, I leaned further. I felt the smoke piercing me as he exhaled the last puff right there, by my lips. I leaned further and inhaled all of, and in no moment, we were too close to resist. We kissed. I didn't know if it was the whiskey, joint, or whatever but I loosened up and I loved every second of it. The very next moment I was on top of him smooching him as he sat there kissing me breathlessly whilst I unbuttoned his shirt.

With our tongues swirling inside others' and hands hovering over each others' bare skin by the time we realised that we were in the hall, we were already half-naked. He hooked my bra back and showed me his room. I saw him picking up the condoms from below the cushion.

He came in and locked the door behind and the next moment pushed me on the wall, and kissed my neck, fondling my breasts, while I stood there trembling in the warmth of pleasure and joy. I could feel him unhooking my bra as he ran his fingers behind and the very next moment, I pushed him on the bed and vanquished him, kissing his chest, running my lips around his bare body.

There was a diminished flare inside me which just blazed with the erotic touch of his, it was the night of passion where I wanted to conquer the whole world.

I woke up at 1:00 in the afternoon. I just opened my eyes and was astonished to see Gaurav sleeping beside me. I peeked under the sheets, I was just in my lingerie. I felt naked, ashamed. I got up, dressed, and walked out slowly making sure nobody saw me. I reached Neha's apartment.

I was still shaken by everything that happened. Yes, I remember everything, but now after everything that had occurred, it felt like it was the worst decision of my life. I just wanted to hide my face and leave the city. I felt like a slut. I had no idea this one decision would affect me so adversely. I was a virgin and had always regretted the fact that I was entering my late 20s but and never got to live any of it, but now after last night, I was regretting every decision of mine, even my decision to come to Mumbai.

Neha and Ananya came back to the apartment later, I was there in the room, sleeping with my face covered face down, tears staining my cheeks. I didn't even know when I fell asleep.

"*Deepti, what happened? Tell me.*" Neha asked as she held my hand and sat beside me.

I just felt ashamed, I started crying again. I just told them everything in my broken voice.

"*I feel like a slut. I had sex with a guy whom I met for the first time.*"

"*I didn't even know what to do, I woke up and simply walked out of the room. I am just wondering what it's going to look like.*"

"*Deepti, it's never about that. You didn't do anything wrong.*" Ananya said, gently caressing my hands while I leaned on Neha's shoulder.

"*You did what you liked at the moment, and it's not wrong. He is a good guy and you know that. Just talk to him, things will be fine.*" They consoled me for almost an hour, I felt a bit better, but I was still ashamed of what happened.

It was 11 at night when we were all done with dinner. I was feeling slightly better after all the conversations and everything, but I still felt hollow from the inside. It was eating me from beneath.

They planned to meet up with the guys again and asked me to meet with Gaurav and talk about it. They suggested that he is a sensible guy and talking might help, but I was in no mood to talk to him or even face him. I was too ashamed to go in front of him.

They left the apartment and went to theirs, as I told them I will join later.

Just after a few minutes, I dropped a message to Neha.

"*Hey Neha. I am just going out for a while. Please don't worry, I need to be alone for some time, I will be back soon.*"

It was 11:30. I booked a cab and set the destination as Marine Drive. I didn't know about the place much, but I had heard it was serene at night.

In no time, I was in a cab.

Aarav

It was morning. I woke up with a slight headache after the night of the party. Shruti had already left. It was a bit surprising for me as she didn't even inform me or drop a text.

I dropped her a text and went to freshen up. I had a meeting scheduled in an hour.

It was 10:30 when I reached the office, Mira was already there.

"*Morning Mira.*"

"*Good morning sir*" She replied bluntly.

I thought to talk to her about last night, but I had three meetings scheduled back to back and had a really hectic day.

It was almost 7 in the evening when I was done with the meetings. I checked my phone again for any of Shruti's message, but there was none. I tried calling her once or twice but couldn't reach her. I wasn't sure what last night was about, but I was looking forward to asking her out.

"*Mira, do you have a minute. Please?*" I asked her as I saw her prepping up to leave the office for the day.

"*Sure, sir*" She said. I asked her to take a seat.

"*It's not about our work and anyways your office hours are over so no need for formalities.*" I said with a smile.

She nodded. I could see the slight discomfort on her face.

"*I am sorry that we got interrupted yesterday, but it was a good conversation. I had a great time with you.*"

"*I really wanted to thank you for everything that you have done for me so far.*" I continued.

"*Thank you, Aarav!*" She said with a smile.

My phone beeped the very next moment. I ignored it. The next second I heard it beeping continuously, and so was Mira's. We both looked at our phone. There were messages from numerous contacts.

The very next moment I saw Mira expression turn grave. Before I could check the messages, she stood up and grabbed my phone from my hand.

"*Let's go out somewhere.*" She said as she put my phone in her bag.

"*What is it Mira, what happened?*" I asked. I was surprised at the way she was behaving.

"*Nothing, you said we had a good time yesterday. If you don't mind can we have dinner together today?*" She said as she packed my laptop and iPad and kept the bag with herself.

She was standing at the door waiting for me.

"*Umm okay!*" I said. I took my blazer and headed out of the door.

We left the building and then left for my apartment as she suggested that she didn't want to go out today.

We reached my place by 8:00. Mira had my chef prepare a meal for two. We dined together while she still had my phone hidden in her purse on silent mode. I asked her a few times, but she just changed the topic.

Finally, we were done with the meal and a few glasses of wine, and now we were sitting on the porch watching the city from the top.

"*Mira, can I have my phone now. Please!*" I asked her.

"*Aarav, I want to tell you something.*" She said as she held my hand gently.

I looked at her. I just stood there still thinking about everything that happened yesterday. It was all coming off as a blur.

There was a pause. We just looked into each other's eyes. She had been working for me for more than five years now, though sometimes I felt that there was something more as she always cared for me a little too much, but she never expressed. If I say I had none, I wouldn't be saying the truth, but I had always suppressed it. It was work and I would never mess it up.

We sat there holding hands, looking at each other. I didn't know what to say, I choose to stay quiet.

She broke the silence.

"*Aarav, I know it's going to be weird, but I guess now is the right time.*"

"*We had the perfect, most professional relation, you have been by my side most of the time, whenever I was in a crisis or needed anything.*"

She continued…

"*I just want you to know that I am here for you, whenever you need me and whatever comes around.*"

"*I mean it.*" She said and she hugged me.

We hugged.

I felt the warmth of her hug, she held me tight. I got lost into her, but the next moment I realised what happened last night with Shruti and I felt bad about it. I somewhere knew that Mira liked me but I never talked to her about it.

With the cluster of thoughts clouding my mind, I was totally overwhelmed to know what was right and what was not. The very moment I heard a knock over the door.

We went inside the hall to see one of my household standing there.

"*Yes?*" I said looking at him as this was unusual for him to knock while I was with someone.

"*Sir, there were some people coming to visit but as Mira mam had asked me not to let anyone. I didn't.*" He said. I turned around and looked at Mira. She was frowning.

"*Sir, they have asked me to tell you to check your phone. It's urgent.*" He said again. It felt like I just woke up, I had totally forgotten about my phone since I was with her.

"*Mira, I need my phone*" I said. Her face went pale. She slowly took out the phone from her purse and walked to me.

"*Aarav, please sit down.*" She said and pushed me slowly on the couch beside.

"*Take it easy, whatever it is. I am here right beside you.*" She said quietly and handed me the phone.

I unlocked it. I was shocked at the sight. There were 25 missed calls and more than 100 messages. I opened the messages while Mira held my hand.

I wasn't sure what was happening until I opened my first message. I was in shock. I couldn't believe my eyes. There were pictures of me and Shruti from the last night, uncensored pictures. I checked the other messages, all of them had links of social media blogs and screenshot from different websites with pictures of me and Shruti and some framed story.

I scrolled down. There was a message from Shruti.

"*Just thought to give you a heads up, it was me, and btw last night was fun :P*"

I was just shunned at the moment. I was filled with rage. I checked the calls. There were calls from my investors, clients, employees.

"*She just fucked everything.*" I shouted. I slammed my phone hard on the floor.

I was out of my mind. I just didn't know what to do, how to react. It felt like I had my whole life shattered right in front of me.

"*Aarav, we will sort this together. I will help you with every step, I have already made some calls.*" Mira said as she held my hand.

"*Mira, I messed up everything. I was there talking to you, having the perfect moment and then she came, and well here I am, fucking loser.*" I almost shouted.

"*I made this choice Mira and trust me I know I would regret this for my whole life.*" I was shattered realising whatever I had been looking for years to fill the void in my heart, was right beside me and then for one night I just toppled it all.

"*Nothing's changed Aarav, whatever it is there doesn't bother me. I love you Aarav, I still love you.*" She said as I could see a tear running down her eyes.

"*I don't deserve you, Mira.*" I just said and left the hall picking up a random car key from the tray.

"*Please, I need to be alone.*" I left and headed to the elevator.

There I was whirring my convertible BMW through the roads of Mumbai. I was shattered, and ashamed for the thing that I just lost. I might have never admitted to myself, but I knew Mira was a gem for me, and no one could have filled that void.

I still had some content of alchohol as I could feel it while the cold breeze brushed my face. I was trying my best not to put it out on the accelerator as I was already speeding up.

After driving around, speeding through the streets, having the lone time, I soothed down a bit. I drove off to Marine Drive. It was one of the places where I had always gone on the days when I wanted to be alone.

It was almost midnight. I parked my car at one empty corner of the Marine Drive. I wanted a peaceful spot, an empty one.

WHEN THEY MET

Deepti was sitting in one empty corner of the Marine Drive. She was just staring at the waves hitting the shore, whilst the moonlight dipped the waves into the silver sheet. Her eyes were still damp, and she was shedding tears alone, judging herself with every breath she took. It felt different to her, and she had no idea how to face it or forget it.

She heard a car engine roar from behind. She turned back and saw some sports convertible car parked just a few feet away. A guy came out in a suit and walked past her.

Aarav sat on one corner, just a few feet away from her.

He remembered the first time he couldn't land a job, he came here at the same spot and was there until it was time for the last local. This was the place with which he has shared a lot of falls and numerous successes. The endless bay with the streetlights wrapping it, the sea waves hitting the rocks and the far off lights glimmering on some distant boats, was just the perfect place for solitude. He just used to sit there and listen to the waves hitting the rocks. There was some kind of melody that has kept him glued to this place. Not only him but thousands of people who come there either to share their story in solace or to find a new one.

He just sat there listening to the waves with his hands grasping his head. It was burning, he was filled with anger, rage, regret. He was embarrassed for his poor judgment and the fact that he trusted Shruti. It was the regrets and the mistakes that had clouded him at the moment and with every wave hitting hard, he was reminded of each one of them. His company's name was on stake and so was his reputation, and on the other hand, he had no idea how to face Mira again after all of this. The fact that she cared so much for him made it worse.

He was lost in his thoughts when he heard something. He turned around. It was the girl sobbing, the girl who was sitting just a few feet away. He looked at her while she had her face covered with her hands. He could hear her heavy breaths.

He ignored and sat there, staring at the darkness of the ocean which laid right beside the shining city. He checked for his phone in his pocket, but it wasn't there. He remembered that he had smashed it in his apartment.

Deepti's phone started ringing. She wiped her tears as she pulled out the phone from the pocket. She looked at the screen. She kept staring at the screen while the phone was still ringing, the very next moment she threw her mobile phone in the ocean.

Aarav saw everything, he was perplexed to see her throw her phone. He was just looking at her as she covered her face again and this time her sob was even louder. He could see her trembling and wiping off her tears.

Aarav just took off his blazer and moved towards her and handed her slowly. She looked at him with the face of denial, but she knew she needed it. She just nodded and took it from him and wrapped herself in the blazer. They sat there together without exchanging any words. She still had her face buried, crying while Aarav was still fogged with the thoughts in his mind.

"*Do you have a phone? I need to make a call.*" She asked Aarav in a broken voice, somehow collecting the words together.

"*Umm… Actually, I don't have. Was it urgent?*" Aarav asked.

"*That's okay.*" She responded.

"*What is it? If you don't mind you can share.*" He asked.

"*Nothing much just had a bad day.*" She said hesitantly.

There was a pause again, they just sat there looking at the ocean.

"*What about you? You are sitting here alone, that too in a suit?*" She broke the silence.

"*Well, I kind of messed up.*" Aarav said.

"*If you would be having your phone with you, you would have known by now.*" He added.

"*Are you a celeb or what?*" She asked as she looked at him and then at his car.

"*Umm, I don't know. I wish I wasn't.*" He chuckled.

"*I slept with someone and well, she is a journo and now she has faked a story and has leaked our pictures. It's all over social media.*" He said with a sigh.

"*I lost my reputation, my company's name and well, I guess someone who is dear to me.*" He continued.

"*No doubt it's Mumbai.*" She said.

"*Sorry, what?*" Aarav looked at her and asked as he couldn't understand where it came from.

"*Well, you slept with someone and now you are telling me about it, a complete stranger. No doubt everything is just so casual here.*" She said abruptly.

Aarav sighed and took a pause.

"*Uhh… Yeah, I know. Looks like you are having a hard time here.*" He said while still measuring every word he said.

"*I am sorry, I didn't mean to judge you. But yeah, kinda.*" She replied.

"*That's okay. Well, isn't this the best thing about being strangers, we won't judge each other. Like, we don't even know each other's name.*" He said looking at her.

She nodded with acceptance.

"*So, what is it about you?*" Aarav asked her.

She sighed, and told him everything.

"*It might not be a big deal for you, but I have lived a different life and this is totally new to me.*" She added.

"*I understand you totally.*"

"*And trust me, most of the people here are pretending to be casual about everything, they are all messed up inside.*" Aarav added.

"*Well, I kind of tried being casual about a lot of things lately. Doesn't seem to please me anymore.*"

"*Or maybe it's just the short-lived pleasure.*" She added.

"*Yeah, people here have been living for these short-lived pleasures now, cause I guess they are done with complications, feelings, being left out, and loneliness.*" Aarav replied.

"*Aren't all of these emotions just make us humane?*" She asked.

"*Yeah they do, but people are tired of being humane.*"

"*You know, life in cities like this are quite complicated. Everyone here is to fulfil their dream, chase their passion. Almost every people around are being shouted at, bullied, insulted, broken, shattered. I don't say this is right or wrong but in a way, they just found a way to find peace with a few things and not to complicate it.*"

"*Life is already quite complicated, sometimes along all the chaos people pause their emotions and bury it deep inside, just to have some good time and cherish it while they are onto it.*" Aarav finished, as she looked at his watch. It was almost 1:30.

"*Maybe you are right.*" She whispered.

"*Whatever it is that's bothering you, if you felt it to be right at the moment then don't think about it.*" Aarav said.

"*Nothing is always sorted in life. We just learn to live with it.*" He added.

She nodded.

They didn't speak for the rest of the time, all they could hear was the waves roaring, piercing through the rocks. It was a rewind for both of them to look into their lives and realise what really matters and what is that they really want out of it. You can never carry on with everything at a time, you will always lose something.

Deepti had always fascinated about the urban social life but when she was breathing in it, she was suffocating. She even wasn't sure if she liked it or not, all she knew was the burden of the regrets that was dragging her behind. She had to sort it out. If she liked it, she should let go off the regrets that she was carrying and if she didn't, she needs to forget it and move on. At least she won't carry the regret of not knowing what it feels like to live such a life.

Aarav always had a clear goal about his career and accomplishments that he never got time to look into his personal life. With the work and professionalism, he had kept his romantic life on the backseat and forgot how it felt to be loved. Yes, he did make a big mistake, but the good thing was it made him realise what he had been hiding from himself for a long time, his admiration for Mira.

"*It's late, I guess. I need to head back. My friends must be worried.*" She said looking at her watch, it was almost 2 a.m.

"*Yeah, it is.*" Aarav said as he realised it was quite late.

"*Shit, I don't even have my phone to book a cab.*" She murmured in disgust, as she recalled she threw her phone away.

"*Don't worry, I will drop you. Hope you know the address.*" He said.

"*Thanks!*" She murmured.

She told him the society name and the location, the most of it that she remembered. They both talked about everything while he drove around the city at midnight searching for her place. After almost an hour they reached her society complex.

"*You should call your friend downstairs first.*" Aarav went and talked to the security guard. They made a call to their apartment.

"*They will be here in ten*" Aarav said as he opened the gate of his car for her.

"*Thanks a lot for everything.*" She said.

He nodded.

"*Hey Deepti, where were you? We were sick worried.*" Neha shouted from the other side of the gate.

Deepti breathed a sigh of relief as she saw her, and hugged her tight.

She walked to Aarav to bid him bye and shook hands.

"*In case you plan to embrace this city's life, howsoever it be, this is my office's number. Just walk by, for a job.*" He smiled as he handed her a piece of paper.

"*Wow, thanks a lot.*" She exclaimed. She was surprised by his gesture.

"*Hope you sort out your things as well.*"

"*And no matter what happens, hold onto the ones by your side.*" She said, he nodded with a smile.

Deepti turned back and went inside the society complex. She saw someone standing on the other side. Before she could say anything, she saw him walking towards her.

It was Gaurav. He came forward and hugged her. She just stood there surprised while a smile appeared on her face. It was the comfort that soothed her, for she realised that sometimes everything is not what it really appears to be.

"I am sorry for everything, but you need to know; I like you" He whispered.

Aarav walked back to his car and zipped off to his apartment.

There was Mira still sitting on the couch, waiting for him. He could see the tear marks on her face. He just walked to her and before she could say anything, he pulled her in his arms and kissed her.

She was startled. She had to say a lot of things and ask a lot of questions but this time she knew that Aarav too has a lot to say.

"*Mira, I love you.*" Aarav said, bending there on his knees with a rose in his hand and asked. "*Mira, will you be with me forever.*"

Mira was blushing with her smile widening every second. She had tears in her eyes, though this time it was the joy that made her cry. She had been waiting for this for years and now all of her dreams were right in front of her.

"*Yes, Aarav. I love you too. And yes, I will always be there with you.*" She held his hand took the rose and kissed him. Kissed him as if the moment froze and the night was just warm and long.

It was love that finally crawled out of their hearts into each others'.

THE TOXIC LOVE

Aneesh

I kept pressing the doorbell button waiting for Ritu to open the door. With the laptop bag on one shoulder and my lunch pack on the other, and after a long day and a tiring drive, I was feeling frustrated.

She rushed and opened the door, I barged in, threw the bag on the couch and started taking off my shoes.

"Where the hell were you, I was waiting outside for more than five minutes." I snapped, my voice rising as I walked toward the bathroom to freshen up.

"Baby I was in the washroom, sorry you had to wait." She pleaded following me to the bathroom.

"You don't have anything to do, not even a job. The least you can do is help me out." I muttered, still simmering with anger.

She walked away slowly and headed to the kitchen. She knew extending this conversation any further would get ugly.

Her eyes were moist but she took a long breath and settled into a corner. Across the kitchen, in another room sat my mother, scrolling through her mobile phone. Ritu was visibly irritated because my mother didn't get the door for me while she was unavailable.

I walked to mom's room, as I often spent some time with her after work. I sat with her chatting about the day. The next moment I saw her get up from the bed, as she went and shut the door of the room. She realised that Ritu might overhear us, as this room was adjacent to the kitchen.

"I don't understand what she does the entire day. She is not working as well now, she got kicked out of her job. For cooking also, she asked you to not let go of the maid, I don't know what does she want."

I listened to my mother while she complained about Ritu. I knew they had differences, especially since she had moved in with us. Ritu of course does not understand her well, and has been a bit rebellious about a few things, but obviously I can't say anything to my mom, and she doesn't seem to understand this. She will have to adjust, there's no other way.

"Maa, that was layoff. It's going on in several companies these days, it's not that she is incompetent. It can happen to anyone." I replied gently to her. I knew this was nowhere her fault as things haven't been going well in corporate these days.

"Yeah, now you will take her side. That is what she wants. She doesn't work, can't even cook and just want to rest in the house." She said angrily.

"I have already asked the maid to not cook anymore, since Ritu is at home now a days, she can do some basic things right." She added further.

I looked at her, a bit surprised as we did not discuss about this earlier. Although I understand how she looks at things, and Ritu definitely has got time in her hands since she hasn't been working lately.

"And son, I know she is not in your control anymore. She didn't even ask me, and bought some tablet, iPad for herself."

"You are just wasting your money, if you want to burn it all, just hand it over I will do it. She is not earning, doesn't want to do anything and now she is spending money recklessly."

She abruptly poured everything out on me. I just sat there listening to her. I knew about the iPad, she had it planned for her business venture she wanted to start. I wanted to tell my mom, but I could feel her rage and if I would have said anything at that moment, she would have rebuked me for taking her side.

I heard a knock on the door, it was Ritu.

"Dinner is ready." She said with a straight face and walked out shutting the door behind. I knew she must

have overheard things, and she didn't like it, but I was the one getting stuck in between the two.

"Oh god, she doesn't even let us talk."

"Go son, your wife has prepared dinner for the first time in the house." Mom said, taunting me. I knew she was pissed. I held her by her shoulder and convinced her to come out for dinner.

We sat around the dinner table, dinner was served. Ritu and I sat on one side and mom opposite to us.

"How much is that tab that you got?" Mom asked Ritu, as she took another bite of the chapati.

Ritu hesitated, as she knew she would freak out after knowing the price.

She asked again with her brows raised. I looked at her, staring at Ritu with her brows raised, and eyes wide open.

"It's around forty Maa." Ritu replied, looking at me. I knew she was expecting me to intervene, and try and stop mom, but this wasn't going to help either of us. I knew my mom, she was already convinced that I am taking Ritu's side more than often. If I would have interrupted, things would have just escalated.

"Forty thousand?" She repeated the words in awe. She was in a shock.

"You spent so much, do you even ask for permission. You are not even working." She shouted loudly.

"Maa, I had saved for it and, I have told Aneesh about….." Before Ritu could complete her sentence.

"You are totally out of hands now."

"What do you mean, your savings."

"You should have taken permission from me."

"You are wasting my sons hard earned money, he is doing everything for you, and you say it is your money, you were saving for it." Mom's voice rose with every word she uttered.

I saw Ritu's eyes, she was barely able to hide her tears.

"Maa, I needed it, that's why I bought." Ritu said, her voice quivering.

"And she is arguing now, this is the manner that she has." My mum shouted getting up from the table. She pushed her plate away.

"Aneesh, better get my ticket to go home, I will rather live alone there than here, where I am not respected." She

added furiously. Her face turned red reflecting her temper with every word she uttered. She walked off and left the room angrily.

"Ritu, what are you doing? You shouldn't be talking to her like that!" I turned to Ritu. I felt irritated by the way she talked to mom as it felt wrong. After all, she is my mother, she shouldn't be talking to her like that. She needs to learn to let go of a few things.

"Aneesh, if you can't stand up for me, I will have to. I am doing everything to please her but she doesn't care. When I was working she had issues, now that I am not she still has issues."

"What should I really do to please her?" I could see tears running down her cheeks .

"I don't want to eat, you go on." I banged my fist on the table and left. My frustration was at its peak. This has been like an everyday thing now, and I was always the one standing in between them. Mom, obviously I can't change her, and Ritu does not even try to understand.

I heard her weeping in the bedroom. With mom in one and Ritu in another, I was too pissed to talk to anyone at that moment.

I walked to the drawing room, took a cushion and slept there itself.

It was 7 in the morning, and I was already awake. Ritu was in the kitchen while mum was still asleep.

I checked my phone for the ride sharing app, that I often use, while going to work.

Basically it's an app where people going to offices through similar routes as yours, can join you. They pay a small fee which is cheaper for them as compared to cabs, and well, ride givers like me, get the fuel share. It's a win win for both.

I saw a request, it was from Aditi.

She was a frequent rider, so I accepted it without a second thought, locked my phone and started getting ready. Meanwhile Ritu had the breakfast ready and was packing lunch for me.

ADITI

After two long days of continuous travel, I was not in a condition to sit back and chatter. I got up, said bye to everyone and walked towards my room. It was past midnight and we were supposed to leave early morning the next day.

We were in Goa for the last three days, and I was already waiting eagerly to get back to Mumbai, to sleep on my own bed in my apartment. The level of socialising I had to do in the last few days was enough for the whole month, and now all I wanted was to be left alone, in isolation.

It was a retreat for completion of a project. I am relatively new in my career. This is my first job and I have completed one year in this company. So, this was all new to me, socialising with the teammates outside of work, and balancing professionalism at the same time was definitely tough.

I had mixed feelings about this retreat. I had a good time but there were definitely times when I regretted being here. Well, there's a guy who hasn't been very appropriate to me, his gestures and random touches were totally in bad taste. I didn't like it but I didn't really know what to do. I was thinking if I should mention it to someone or if I should let it go. Those touches were intentional that I knew for sure, but me being new, and him being an old employee and a friend of almost everyone, I already knew people would side with him.

I switched off the lights, pulled the sheet over me, and tried to sleep but these thoughts kept me restless.

We were halfway to Mumbai, and I was already sleepy since I barely slept last night. We had three cars and around twelve people on this trip, and I made sure I sat in a different car than him. I wasn't in the mood to be anywhere near him. By the way, he's Akshay.

"Hey Aditi, I have tagged you in the stories. Please do reshare." I heard a voice from behind. It was Anjali, and she's a social media buff. I can bet she must have clicked a thousand pictures in just the last three days.

"Yeah sure, will do." I replied with a grin, as I pulled my phone out of my jeans pocket. There were a few stories I was tagged in. I just reshared each one of them without bothering to check how I looked. I was sure she must have just looked at herself, and picked the best ones.

It was almost night when I reached my apartment. We already had dinner on the way, so now all I had to do was throw my bags, freshen up and get ten to twelve hours of undisturbed sleep. I really really needed it.

I woke up to a loud knock on my door. Someone was banging it continuously. I checked the time, it was 8 in the morning. I hurried out of the bed, pulling an over shirt from the shelf on the side, to cover my tank top, that I had on.

I stood there surprised, as I swung opened the door. I was unable to process what I saw. Harsh was standing there, right in front of me.

Harsh is my ex, we broke up almost six months ago. I haven't even talked to him in the last couple of months. I had no idea what he was doing here.

"This is what you are doing here?"

"You slut, this is why you got this job in Mumbai, you wanted to be a whore here." He shouted as he barged into my apartment, pushing me aside.

I stood there dumbstruck, I had no idea what he was talking about. Last I knew, he wasn't even living in Mumbai.

"What the hell are you talking about, and what are you doing here?" I shouted as he started throwing my stuff around.

"What happened? You are asking me…, bitch?"

"You went to Goa to fuck around with guys from your office, and you are asking me what happened?"

"I always knew you were a slut." He shouted as he grabbed me by my arm.

I had tears in my eyes. His grip got tighter with every word he uttered. I tried to free myself but the harder I tried, the stronger his grip got.

"You are going to break my hand, what the fuck are you doing" I begged as my arms went sore and the pain got unbearable.

He let go of my arm and shoved me backwards onto the bed. He pulled out the phone from his pocket and threw it on me. I glanced at the screen, it was a picture from one of my stories. It was Akshay standing beside me with his hand around my waist.

"What the fuck is wrong with you? He is the guy who fucking bothered me during the whole trip, and I didn't even know there was a picture like this. I just shared it without even checking" I yelled at the top of my lungs, cornering myself on the other side of the bed to keep him away.

"I am sure you liked it. You whore" He shouted and threw the water bottle kept on the table, on the side.

It hit me on my legs, I was shivering, tears running down my eyes.

I crawled out of the bed slowly as my whole body ached, I was unable to even stand. I looked at him, staring like a maniac.

Before I could manage to stand, he slammed the door, as he walked out, and left.

I stood there whimpering, leaning on the wall, tears running down my eyes. It all came like a nightmare and shook the ground beneath me. I somehow left my past, my toxic, abusive boyfriend and moved to a new city to create a life for myself, but here I am living all of it again. If felt like I was bound with chains, wandering around the field which was never ending. I felt free, but I never was. I felt helpless, trapped, knowing that this was never going to end.

With my arms bruised and leg sprained, barely able to stand, all I had were questions, and so many. The last three days during the trip which were already haunting me and now this. I so desperately wanted to get out of all of this, but I didn't have the courage anymore.

WHEN THEY MET

Aneesh stopped at the location where he was supposed to pick up Aditi. He waited for a minute, looking around trying to spot her.

He heard a knock on the door. It was her.

"Hey, good morning!" Aneesh greeted her, as he unlocked the door .

"Good morning" She mumbled, as she took the passenger seat.

Aneesh glanced at her a few times, but she seemed unusually quiet. The first time when she had joined his drive, she literally spoke nonstop for the entire time. Aneesh knew half of her life stories in just first two hours that he had spent with her. It's been a while since they did ride share but she always had been the talkative and jolly type.

"Hey, you okay?" He asked, as they reached almost halfway and barely had a conversation.

"Yeah yeah, I am fine. Just not feeling great." She replied with a smile.

Aneesh sensed that there was something going on but he didn't ask her again as he didn't want to intrude.

He was still a stranger even though they were kind of friends.

He dropped her on the way to his office, and headed towards his.

It was almost seven in the evening when he got a text, it was from Aditi.

"Hey, you left already?" She asked

"No, I am almost winding up my work, will leave in ten minutes" He replied.

"Oh, I didn't see your ride on the app so thought you had already left."

"No no, I was busy at work, so I forgot to post it. I will ping you once I start from my office." He replied, and got back to his last on call meeting of the day.

They shared their numbers in the initial days itself, but the conversations always had been succinct and formal unlike during the drive, when they were like buddies, cracking jokes, vibing to music together, sharing their days, sometimes grabbing a meal together, or a coffee.

"Hey, I am leaving now." Aneesh dropped a message to Aditi as he turned on the ignition of his car and put on his favourite playlist.

Aditi's office was just five minutes away from his. By the time she replied, he was already there. He parked his car on the side and waited for her.

After a few minutes, he saw her walking towards the car, slightly limping. He started the car and drove as close to the office gate as he could.

"Hey, thank you so much!" She said stepping inside the car as she saw him getting the car closer to her.

"I am sorry you had to wait" She added.

"Hey, don't worry! I was just browsing my playlist." Aneesh replied with a giggle.

"The traffic looks bad today. It's already showing two hours." He said pointing to the map on his car as they drove off.

It was already an hour and there were just few words exchanged. It started raining heavily and the traffic got worse. Their car stood standstill for almost half an hour as traffic came to a compete halt.

Aditi took off her jacket while adjusting the vents of the car.

"Guess it's not the season for jackets yet." He said with a laugh as he reduced the temperature of the AC. The

very moment he noticed a wound on her shoulder and a bruise on her left arm.

"Hey, I don't want to intrude, but what's going on? What are these marks on your body?" He asked subtly, as his eyes glued to her wounds.

Aditi put the jacket back on, covered herself again, laughed nervously and simply gave an excuse.

"Uhh, nothing, I tripped on the beach. It happened in Goa, I mentioned you earlier na we were going there, the whole team."

Aneesh was somewhat annoyed, he knew she was lying. He cared for her, she was young, just starting her career right after college. He often helped her navigate through her profession life, even her personal front a few times, but this just made him upset. Seeing the wounds, the way she's been talking, her being aloof, he knew there was definitely something going on with her, and he genuinely wanted to help her.

"Oh c'mon, I know you are lying." He replied, annoyed, a clear disbelief written across his face.

"I know, we are not close friends, or I am not your buddy. But I do care for you, and I am, well, quite older than you and therefore I understand the world slightly better,

so I can help you out if there's anything you need help with." He gushed out.

"Tell me what's going on?" He asked again, as he was is no mood to listen to any more lies or excuses.

She looked at him, she knew he wasn't going to let it go. Somewhere deep down she wanted to pour it out to him as it was eating her from inside, she had no one else whom she could talk to.

She took a long pause, battling the thoughts that had her restless for a few days.

"Well, it's a long one, Aneesh" She said, turning to him, looking into his eyes.

"I am all ears, I am not going anywhere" He replied pulling over the car to the side.

She took a long breath, gasped and poured out everything to him. He sat there listening to her each and every words, he was fuming on the inside but kept a straight face the whole time.

She told him about the trip, Akshay's inappropriate behaviour, and then Harsh coming to her apartment, and everything that happened that day.

She also told him about the abusive relationship with Harsh, about the torment that she had to endure in her past times. She told him about the times when he leeched on her money after she landed her job. She told him about the expensive gifts she gave him, about the loan he took from her, about the latest iPhone that he bought using her credit card and never returned back a single penny.

Aneesh kept his calm till the very end. His eyes were furious, but his words softened every time he looked into her eyes. He wanted to hold her hand, hug her, and tell her that the world is cruel, and she has to be strong in order to survive.

"Aditi, don't ever be a victim, and don't ever accept what you don't want to. The world is evil, and if you let down your guard once, you won't be able to lift it up easily." He said, as he tapped on her shoulder.

He could see her eyes turn moist.

"Let's sort it one by one" He said, as he clenched his palm on her shoulder. She was on there verge of breaking down.

"Do one thing, call Akshay now, and simply tell him that his actions made you uncomfortable and it isn't acceptable. If he ever tries that again, there will be consequences."

He looked at her, as he repeated the sentence again.

She was in shock, she was not ready for this. She did not have enough courage to stand up to him and say it out loud.

"Do it now, or else this will keep going now." He said again, this time his voice rose again slightly.

She unlocked her phone, clicked on his contact, it was ringing.

He didn't pick up the call.

"Call again" Aneesh said.

She called again, and this time he answered the call.

"Hi Akshay, this is Aditi."

She said with a soft tone. Anish saw her mumbling, she was barely able to keep her voice high. Aneesh grabbed the phone from her hand, put it on mute and said, *" You are not calling him for a casual chat, be fucking strict."*

"If you want I can talk to him." He said looking at her, slightly agitated.

She took the phone again, unmuted it and started speaking. She gathered all the courage that she had and started spitting the words.

"Akshay what happened during the trip is unacceptable and I didn't like it."

Aneesh put the phone on speakerphone.

"I didn't mean anything Aditi, you are getting me wrong." He said in an apologetic tone.

"Akshay, I know it was all intentional, I just wanted to tell you that if you ever try this again there will be consequences, and bad ones."

She added, this time her voice grew stronger and louder.

"I am really sorry Aditi, I totally understand"

"I am sorry" He repeated and disconnected the call.

Aneesh looked at her with a smile, she gasped and kept the phone aside. She looked happier, she felt lighter, her face lit up with a smile.

"Feeling better?" Aneesh asked, looking at her, smiling.

"Much better" She replied with a grin. It was like a victory for her, standing up for herself, for once and having the courage to say it out loud.

"You did good!" Aneesh said.

"Now it's time for the next one." He added looking at her.

Aditi knew what he meant and she was not at all ready for this, she knew what kind of guy Harsh was.

"Aneesh, don't do it, he is a maniac. You don't understand, it can create even a bigger mess for me." She said in a pleading tone, requesting Aneesh not to call Harsh.

"Don't worry Aditi, I will take care of this. I promise you won't be bothered again." Aneesh said, as he unlocked his phone.

"Give me his number" He asked.

She looked at him in surprise, she had no clue what was his plan or what he was going to do.

"Please don't" She almost begged.

"Aditi, do you see yourself, the bruises that he gave you? You really don't want to do anything about them?" He asked her angrily, trying hard to keep his tone down but his temper was surging.

"Let me handle this, it won't escalate. Trust me." He added.

She gave him his number and he dialled it from his phone. It was ringing.

Harsh picked the call.

"Hello" Harsh said.

Aneesh took a long pause.

"Yeah, Mumbai police here. I have received a complaint against you for domestic violence. We are filing an FIR against you." Aneesh uttered these words in the coldest manner that he could.

There was a pause.

"Sir, it was a personal matter, nothing more." Harsh said, he was about to continue further but Aneesh cut him right in the middle.

"This is not personal anymore. I have got the complaint from the building manager also, people have seen what you did. The girl is standing in front of me. I am filing an FIR, this is just to inform you, we will be getting a warrant very soon." Aneesh added.

"Sir, I am really sorry sir. I will never do this again sir. It was a bit mistake from my side. Please don't file FIR sir. I am really sorry." Harsh started pleading. They could feel the fear in his tone, his voice shaking.

Aditi smiled, as she realised what's happening. She felt a sense of relief.

"You have taken loan as well, right?"

"For what.. ummm... iPhone it was, right? The amount is more than a lakh."

"See, there are multiple charges, there is no other way now."

"I am filing the FIR, you will be getting a copy as well."

Aneesh kept on going with his threats, and before he could complete his sentence, he could hear Harsh crying on the phone. He continuously pleaded, begged, to forgive him,

"Sir, give me sometime, I will return all her money." Harsh said, with his voice breaking, sobbing.

"You have 15 mins, the girl is in front of me. Send the whole amount now, if I don't get in 15 mins, we will see you tomorrow with a warrant." Aneesh said this and disconnected the phone.

Aditi was looking at him in awe. She couldn't believe what just happened. Her face was glowing, he could see how relieved she was.

"Sometimes you need to take the hard steps" He said, Aditi nodded.

Aditi received a credit notification on her mobile phone from her bank. It was thirty thousand. She was surprised to see this, though Aneesh was expecting it. He could sense the fear in his voice over the call, he knew he was going to return every penny. In the next few minutes she got a few more deposit messages.

"Wow, I got the whole amount" She almost screamed with joy. She was excited as if she had won a battle.

Yeah, she did. She won a battle for her self-respect, her self-esteem, her scars, and everything she had endured until now.

Aneesh phone started ringing, it was Harsh.

"Sir, I have sent the entire amount sir. Please forgive me sir, please don't file the FIR." He continued pleading.

"You better not even try to reach her again, or come anywhere near her, if I get a sense of anything as such, I will not even wait for a FIR then." Aneesh threatened Harsh, he listened quietly promising to never contact her ever again.

The call disconnected. Aditi was thrilled, she leaned forward and hugged Aneesh.

"Thank you so much Aneesh!" She thanked him from the bottom of her heart, he was like a guardian angel for her today.

"Your wife must be so lucky to have a man like you. I really wish I find such a man, who can stand by me, like you did." She said still smiling at him.

Aneesh sat there, listening to her words.

"I have had such a bad taste in men earlier, that I could never see my own worth, even the bare minimum felt like a blessing. What a fool I was?" She said laughing.

Aditi's words echoed in his mind, "*Your wife must be so lucky to have a man like you*". He sat there listening to Aditi laugh as she said something but all he could think was, was he really a good man? Was he really a good husband?

All these questions stirred him up.

He wondered if Ritu was really happy, especially with everything going on lately after his mother moving in with them. The quarrels, her late night cries, her being targeted for losing her job, him not defending her even when he knew she wasn't wrong, just because he can't take stand of her in front of his mother.

He drove to Aditi's home, dropped her there, bid bye and left for his house. Aditi felt elated as he just made her day, but somehow it made him realise that he hasn't been playing his part well, as a husband, he wasn't putting enough effort or time into it. He couldn't even recall when was the last time when he brought a smile on her face.

"Hey!" He called Ritu. She answered.

"Have you cooked dinner?" He asked, as it was already late due to traffic.

"Yeah, it's almost done." She replied.

"Okay" He took a pause.

"Do one thing, serve it to mom. You get ready, we will go out tonight, let's eat out." He added.

Ritu was surprised to hear this, that he wanted to go out for dinner, just the two of them and not his mum. She couldn't really understand what was going on as they never went out together, alone, since she started living with them.

"Are you sure?" She asked.

"You mean, just us? Like me and you will go for dinner?" She confirmed again as this was almost unbelievable for her.

He laughed. *"Yeah it's just us. Don't worry, I will talk to mom."*

"You just get ready, I will be there in fifteen." He added and then disconnected the call.

Aneesh reached home, Ritu was ready wearing a lovely saree. He looked at her, admiring her beauty, she looked amazing. It was her smile that made her even more charming.

Aneesh walked to the kitchen and started severing the food alongside Ritu. Seeing this, both Ritu and his mom was surprised.

"Beta, why are you in the kitchen?" Aneesh's mom walked into the kitchen, taking the dishes from him.

"Maa, it's not like I can't do this." Before he could complete the sentence, his mom said, *"but you don't need to, you just came from work, let Ritu serve the food."*

"Ritu, what are you doing, standing there and watching?" Mom shouted. Ritu hurried to the kitchen as she heard her.

Aneesh held her mother by her shoulders firmly, and looked at her.

"Maa, listen, I know you care about me, but don't you think, if dad would have also been there for you, helped you with everything, encouraged with your work, you would have also been living your life differently, how you always wanted."

"I am doing this for Ritu, yes, but I am doing all of this mainly because of you maa. I have seen you struggle, taking care of me, our whole joint family. I know you had to leave your job which you always wanted to pursue just because the family didn't support you, not even dad. But now, I don't want the same thing for Ritu, and I am sure maa, you also

don't want the same thing. You know how it feels giving up on your dreams."

"I want you to see a reflection of yourself in her, and help her through her journey maa."

There followed a long silence, Aneesh knew he brought up something very personal to her.

His mother stood there looking at him, a tear ran down her eyes. She was on the verge of breaking down. He took her to a chair, and sat there, hugged her.

"I never wanted to be harsh on Ritu, son" She said in a trembling voice, He held her tight.

"I know maa, I know you don't." He sat there holding her in his arms while she looked at Ritu and made her sit right beside them.

"Beta, I always will always support you with whatever you want to do. I don't want you to have a life like mine, crumbled under all the burden. I don't want you the repeat the same mistakes that I did earlier."

"You have my blessings beta" She said, holding Ritu's hand tightly. Aneesh could see her relieving every moment of her past.

They sat around the table, while his mother ate. They shared laughs and conversations and the night turned jovial. Aneesh and Ritu shared a light meal with her, as they informed they will go out for sometime and might have dinner outside.

Aneesh hugged her mom bye and the walked out of the apartment.

They drove to a lovely five star hotel, Aneesh had a table booked there for dinner. Ritu was still trying to understand everything that had happened this evening, but she was glad.

They sat there, and talked for hours, while eating their favourite food. They discussed Ritu's plan for the venture, that she was planning to start in the interior designing field. She shared some of the ideas that she had, and they shared their perspectives and feedback.

They drove out again, the roads turned empty, and chaos toned down, while the buildings stood tall glimmering with the night lights.

Ritu carried a smile throughout the drive, looking outside the window.

"Where are we going?" Ritu asked as she saw Aneesh going on an unfamiliar route.

Aneesh smiled, *"Well, I thought let's get a chai"*

Ritu giggled in joy, she had been longing for quite some time to see this side of Aneesh. It had vanished totally since the last few months. They barely had a moment together.

He drove to Marina Drive, and parked on the side. They both walked around grabbed a cup of tea each, and sat down alongside the shore.

"I have always loved this place" Aneesh said as he wrapped his arms around her.

Ritu smiled, feeling warm and fuzzy with his arms around her. She was in a fairyland, living her best life. She wanted to live in this moment forever, stay here in each other's arms, watching the waves hit the rocks.

"I am sorry for not being there for you lately."

"I am sorry for not standing up for you"

"And, I am sorry for not taking care of you"

Ritu tried stopping him, but he shushed her with his fingers on her lips.

"I am sorry for not being a good husband". He added.

Ritu already had a tear running down her eyes.

"You are perfect, you don't need to say these." She said hugging him tightly.

He looked at her eyes, as if he was falling in love with her all over again.

He leaned forward and kissed her.

Ritu reciprocated but backed out. She was totally shook.

What are you doing, we are in a public place. She said shying away.

"It's not like we haven't done this before. We still can." He laughed.

He leaned forward and kissed her again. She was hesitant for a bit then she gave away. Ignoring everything around, the sound of couple talking beside, the occasional honks of the cars, the exhaust of bikes racing around, they kissed, immersed into each other, living every second if it, forgetting the world around.

THE LOST DESIRE

KANISHK

It was yet another morning when I woke up alone in my bed. My husband didn't return last night, again. It had been happening quite repeatedly for the last few weeks. Earlier he used to be out once in a fortnight or so. He said it was work and I believed him for a long time until I started looking into things.

We had been married for three years now. Sometimes I wonder if this is even a successful marriage, or just an oppressive one. I don't remember the last time we expressed our love for each other. Well, our relationship didn't even have the spark left anymore. It was long since we sat together and talked about something. I don't even remember the last time when we warmed the bed together. It's been months I could say, and that too because I asked for it desperately. I had to wear the sluttiest nightwear on his drunken nights to feel the love that we lost a long time ago.

I heard a thud on the door. I pulled the cover on my over revealing nightwear that I wore last night and walked out of the room. There he was sneaking inside.

"*You didn't come last night?*" I asked. He ignored me and walked past me. He went inside and directly headed to the shower.

Here we were, the urban married couple. I don't even know what it means, but I wonder if everyone's marriage is so messed up in such big cities with their chaotic life or was it just us. The husband was busy at work, or I guess pretending to be too busy and then there was me, a passionate young lady, who had dreams to live life on her own terms. But in the end, she was just a desperate housewife who needed to be fucked once in a while and made to live on somebody else's choice just to make her realise that she was still married.

I walked to the kitchen and prepared breakfast, just like an ideal wife would do. Yeah, this kind of sums up my life.

I served him breakfast as he took a seat on the dining table.

"*You were busy with work? How's everything?*" I asked as I took a seat beside him.

He ate a few bites and then answered "*Yes, it's been difficult expanding our business. I have to put up a lot of work into it.*"

"*Oh you must be tired, I guess you need some rest.*" I said and poured him some juice.

I heard his phone vibrate. I tried to peek but before I could see anything he flipped over his phone. It vibrated again, and then it started vibrating repeatedly. He took the phone and the glass of juice along and left the table.

"*Kanu I am going to my room. I need some sleep so don't disturb.*" He said as he walked to the other bedroom and locked it from the inside. I just stood there watching him walk away and locking himself in another room.

Things were not the same now. We hardly talked about anything or even sat together for a meal. I was just there to cook for him and serve him. If I ever try to start a conversation, his blunt replies made it clear that he was not even interested to make it work anymore. We were just two strangers living together.

It was evening. I was standing in his room on one side while he was glancing through his wardrobe.

"*You will be late tonight again?*" I asked him as he got dressed.

He nodded, subtly.

His phone vibrated. I looked at it as I heard it fading gradually. It was kept right beside me. I wasn't sure what to do. He didn't notice the vibration. A lot of things were running in my mind, about what should I do and what I shouldn't but before I could think anymore, at the very moment I just pulled a pillow and placed it over the phone.

He didn't notice anything. The next moment he walked inside the washroom. I pulled out the phone slowly and to my luck, it was unlocked.

My heart was racing, I was just too scared to do any of this. Yes, I had wanted this for long, but I wasn't sure if I would be okay to find out whatever it was.

There were a few messages from a number, the contact number wasn't saved. I opened it.

It read.

"*Hey, I will be free for two hours. Come soon!*"

I scrolled and read the next message.

"*I am wearing your favourite saree today, and you won't even guess what's inside.*"

"*Maybe I will drop a clue... something's with one of your favourite colours* 😉"

I was in complete shock. My hands froze, and fingers were hardly responding. I just stood there staring at the mobile screen. I wanted to see more but I was too scared of the reality.

Somehow, I gathered the courage and clicked to check the media files. I was astounded at what I just saw. It was much more than I could have ever thought. I checked the images. I was just petrified to look at them. There he was lying naked with some other women, in some hotel room. There were never-ending pictures of her in different brassieres and thongs, and some nudes of them together. There were some pictures that even I was ashamed to look at.

I heard some noise from the washroom. I was scared to even move, my heart was racing and my fingers were trembling. I had to hide the phone before he comes out and see me going through it. I closed the app, put the phone away, and left the room dazed.

I heard him walk out of the washroom. I tried to catch my breath and made sure I hid all the emotions that I had on my face, at least for the moment.

He walked out of the room, holding his phone. I was just startled to see his face and the rage he carried.

"*What did you just do?*" He asked staring dead at me.

I was horrified. My lips pursed hard together, and my face was running dry.

"*Did you just check my phone?*" He shouted at me.

I was numb. I just stood there still as my body froze. I tried to say something, but the words didn't come out of my mouth. My lips were glued to each other.

"*You read the messages on my phone. How you even dared to touch it?*" He barked at me this time. He walked towards me and pushed me away.

My heart was pacing, and I had no control over my body. All I could hear was the echo of his words repeating in my ears. I somehow managed to turn my face to him but still couldn't utter a single word.

I took a pause, I felt as if I was losing my senses.

"*I didn't read anything. I just touched the screen by mistake.*" I somehow gathered courage and mumbled slowly.

He looked at me, and the very next moment I saw him coming closer.

He pushed me back and he slapped me hard, mercilessly. "*Don't you dare touch my phone again.*" He shouted and pushed me again and left the apartment banging the door behind.

I laid there lying on the floor still wondering what all just happened. My eyes were floating in the tears. It was the first time he ever slapped me, but it was ruthless. I sat there shattered on the floor, crying my heart out.

I woke up after half an hour. As I opened my eyes, I realised I had fallen asleep on the floor itself. I was alone in the home, just like every other day. I got up and walked to my room. I stood in front of the mirror looking at myself, pale and covered with stains of tears. The beautiful lady in her early thirties, who looked almost perfect, the one whom everyone admired once, now was nothing more than a desperate abused housewife.

The mirror showed me more than the stains of the tears. It showed me the reality in which I had been living for long. I didn't want to be that lady, whatsoever I was right then, broken and helpless. I had never imagined myself living such a life. I was just frustrated and wanted to change it right then.

I washed my face trying to clean the smudged mascara along with the stains of the tears. I walked to my wardrobe and pulled out one of my favourite black dress. I tried it out. It fitted perfectly.

I was looking perfect in those black shoes with the short black dress. I stood there admiring myself, but I knew that this happy face and the sexy dress was just a façade that I was carrying to envelop the fact that I was broken inside.

ANSHIT

It's been three years since we broke up but I still couldn't move on. Almost every day she appears in my mind despite the fact that whatever happened years back left me shattered. It was the beginning of my career and I was already a mess with all the things that I had on my plate, and then she asked me for marriage that I just couldn't afford at that time, and I was pretty sure about it.

It was a bare beginning of my paycheques and was too early for me to marry. I couldn't agree to the marriage and seemed like she didn't want to wait. It just went by, she got married to someone else, moved on, shifted to a new city, starting a good life. And here I was, having sleepless nights, crying alone in my room, shutting the world away.

After a long streak of empty nights and glum days, when I finally tried to meet someone new, I just couldn't click. I couldn't feel the warmth again, I didn't have the strength of restarting it all again.

I couldn't get to anything serious except for the few one-night flings that I indulged in. No, it wasn't usual for me. It took me almost two years to get along with any other girl, even in bed. I somewhat knew that the void in my heart would never be filled and I wouldn't be able to mingle romantically anytime sooner.

Well, I just moved to Mumbai a month back. I got a much better job, a bigger apartment, a car but I still wasn't comfortable. Of course, life in Delhi was much better as I knew a lot of people, friends, and families there.

I stood there gazing out of my apartment, standing on the balcony on the 14th floor. The sky was painted in red and the whole of the city was crawling at a seemingly higher pace. It had been almost a month since I came to Mumbai, but I knew no one here. I did not socialise with even a single person here, and I literally had to nowhere to go, no one to meet.

"*Burrpppp, burrrpppp*" My phone vibrated, it was my mom. It was another picture of a girl for marriage. She had sent me more than ten pictures in the last three months, either of the daughters of some neighbour, or some far off known people, or sometimes even of daughters of my dad's friends. I told her several times that I didn't want to marry but they had me nudging every now and then to consider. I knew it wouldn't be the right decision for me to marry someone if I can't be emotionally available for her.

Their concern was right, but I just couldn't tell them directly that I still hadn't moved on and I cannot put someone else's life in misery just for the sake of their happiness.

I sat there, on a beanbag in my balcony scrolling through my Insta feed. The very next moment, I paused, locked the phone, and kept it back inside my pocket. I sat there looking at the view, out of the glass fenced balcony. The fast pacing city with people rushing towards their life looked the same every evening.

I pulled out my phone again. I knew I shouldn't be going for it, but I did it, again. I logged into my fake account on Instagram and searched her name. I was glancing at her profile, scrolling through her pictures.

Her feed was filled with the pictures of her recent trip that she took with her husband. I checked the pictures, again and again. There was her husband standing beside her with his hands around her waist.

I logged out and uninstalled the app this time, just to prevent myself from stalking her again. It had been two years, but seeing her picture still stirred something inside me which I thought I had buried long ago. All I could think of was, it could have been me, standing beside her in all of those pictures. Guess I never truly moved on.

I went inside my bedroom and pulled out a bottle of whiskey from the drawer and made a drink. Yes, it had helped me during my lone times, soothing down several sleepless nights.

I was just done from my office and was headed to my apartment. It was a Friday evening after a long and hectic week. I was in no mood to sit back at home tonight. Yes, drinking along with the soothing music on a calm night was a great idea, and but I didn't want to stay home today.

I drove back to my apartment, showered, and got ready to go out. Clubbing was on my mind, as I still hadn't tried any of them in Mumbai. I pulled out my jacket and grabbed my car keys from the tray kept in the hall. I wasn't sure if I should drive as I will have to stay sober to drive back but after trying to find cabs and failing, I finally took the car.

I reached the club by 8:00. I was lucky I got stag entry, it usually gets very difficult to find a good place without any partner. I walked up to a corner in the bar and stood there watching the crowd dancing along with the loud music.

WHEN THEY MET

Anshit stood at the bar as the bartender poured him his first drink. He held the drink as he looked around. It looked as if the whole of the club was dipped in liquor. Everyone around seemed to enjoy the music, grooving to the beats. The changing colourful lights in the dim-lit place made it even more alluring.

He took the drink and walked to the dance floor. He stood at one corner sipping it on the rocks. He looked around when someone caught his sight. The lady on the opposite corner in a black dress. She looked gorgeous. The perfectly wrapped black dress and her long straight hairs that were dangling around her shoulders made her look beautiful. She just stood their sipping a drink, it looked more like a mocktail.

He refrained himself from sharing glances, but he finally gave in, turned around and looked at her again. This time they shared a glance which was longer than usual. While he was trapped in the dilemma if he should approach or not, the very next moment he saw her walk to the dance floor.

Anshit knew there was no harm in starting a conversation. He emptied his glass and kept it on the table by the side and walked to the dance floor. He swayed around, along with the music as he tried to fit in with the drunk dancing crowd. He was just a few feet away from her. She was dancing alone. He saw her trying to rub off the guys dancing around her. As Anshit moved closer, he saw her getting uncomfortable with the two guys. He moved in and joined her, pretending to be together. She reciprocated as the other guys were being real perverts.

Well, it worked. They moved away, and then they were dancing together. "*I hope you didn't mind, I just thought you needed help,*" Anshit said as he moved even closer to her, swaying along with the music.

"*It helped. Thank you!*" She smiled with a nod.

"*I am Anshit by the way.*" He introduced himself as they walked to the middle of the dance floor.

"*Ohh, I am Kanishk.*" The music on the dance floor was growing louder.

"*Sorry, I couldn't hear you.*" Anshit leaned towards her and whispered in her ears.

"*I am Kanishk.*" She replied getting even closer to him, they continued grooving to the tracks.

Anshit got her a drink. She refused initially but then she went for scotch. She knew it wasn't going to be easy for her to pretend everything's okay being sober. She already had a lot on her mind and was somehow trying to push everything away and live in the moment.

"*You want to dance more, or should we take a seat and order something?*" Anshit asked her as he saw her fading away in her thoughts.

"*Ya, let's sit.*" She said and they walked off the dance floor. They took a seat at a corner and ordered some food.

With good food, loud music, and so much to talk about they didn't even realise it was almost two hours since they were sitting together. Anshit told her about his life in Delhi and his new office in Mumbai while Kanishk talked about her college days and told him how she misses everything.

With all the conversation, Kanishk held back the thought of sharing about her marriage. She wasn't sure if she should tell him about it in the first meeting, she wasn't even sure if she was going to meet him again. They had no clue where it was leading to.

It was almost midnight by the time they were done with dinner. He tried to keep the drinks low as he had to drive back.

"*Do you want another drink?*" He asked Kanish as he called for the bill.

She paused and then said "*Yeah, I will just take one more. I guess I need one.*"

"*You don't have to be hard on yourself. Go ahead, order for yourself.*" He chuckled as he ordered another scotch for her.

"*Why aren't you getting another one?*" She asked looking at him. "*Do you have like a few drinks rule?*"

"*No, I don't.*" He laughed.

"*I need to drive back. That's why I am trying to keep it at down.*"

"*Aww, that's sad.*" She said as she sipped her scotch.

"*I know, I should have come by cab.*" He said with his lips curled.

"*What about you? Where are you headed?*" He asked her as we got up and left the table.

"*I live in Andheri, not too far.*" She replied. They walked out of the club now. They were in the open parking.

"*Oh...*" Anshit nodded as they walked to his car.

He wanted to ask her to come over, but he wasn't sure if he should.

"*So, where do you live?*" She asked as they stood by his black SUV.

"*Powai, it's not too far.*" Anshit replied. He was still wondering about what he should do next. He was standing right beside the driver's gate.

"*So, what's up for the night then? You have to go?*" He finally asked gathering all the courage.

He looked at her, she stood there quietly, biting her lips, confused about what really to say. She didn't want to look desperate and neither she wanted to go back to her old life. There was a pause, a long one. He was just wondering if he should have offered to drive her.

She took the leap of courage and broke the silence, "*Nothing as such, no one's waiting.*" She replied with a crisp smile.

"*Oh, okay.*" He sighed of relief.

"*Well, ummm*" He started again but he wasn't sure what to say.

"*Should we go somewhere else, or in case you are tired we can head to my place.*" Anshit asked.

"*It's late now, maybe let's head to your place.*" She replied as he unlocked the car.

The well-lit empty roads with soothing music playing in the car seemed like the perfect midnight drive. Along the drive they talked about a lot of things, she told him about the college and then some of her drunken stories. He told her about his stories of night outs and road trips with his friends, and how badly he was missing Delhi. By the time they reached his apartment, it was almost 1. They were still laughing in the elevator as Kanishk told Anshit about the time she tripped over from her bed and slept there itself for the whole night during her hostel days, while she was drunk.

"*You want some drinks*?" Anshit asked her with a wink as he went inside his bedroom.

"*Really, you have it stocked up?*" She was surprised to see the collection in his drawer.

"*Well, I am a scotch lover. Can't help it.*" Anshit replied as he pulled out a Jack Daniel's bottle from inside the drawer.

"*I am already kinda sobered up, so why not?*" She said with a giggle.

Anshit carried the bottle along with two whiskey glasses and walked to the balcony. He slid the door open and switched on the lights.

It was just the perfect small place to hang out. There were two large bean bags and a small table on which he landed the bottle and the glasses. There was colourful dull lights on both the corners, making it the perfect spot for a soothing date.

"*Damn!*" Kanishk was surprised at what she just saw.

"*You have some pretty good arrangement here. You get company often?*" She asked with a nasty smile.

Anshit laughed. "*No, I don't. You are the first one actually, lucky you han.*"

"*True that.*" Kanishk laughed.

They pulled the beanbags together keeping the table at the side. They sat there facing the blissful beauty, the city lights, and other tall buildings floating around almost everywhere. Those tiny cars were speeding away on the straight laid road.

They sat there taking sips of the swig, whilst a soothing playlist wrapped them together.

"*I am feeling alive after years, I guess.*" Kansihk broke the silence.

Anshit looked at her, staring outside, lost in the music and booze.

He held her hand and leaned closer to her. She turned around and looked into his eyes. He was right there, just a lean away. She could feel his breath as he touched her neck slowly and moved closer. It was warm and dark, his lips smudged on hers and they smooched.

He took the glass from her grasp and put it on the table and the next moment he held her by her waist and kissed her, all over her neck, fondling her skin while she unzipped her dress. He could see her mumbling as his lips caressed her bare skin. They got up and walked to the bedroom, kissing and fondling.

She threw herself on the bed as he followed her there, fondling her flesh and smooching her lips. She enjoyed every bit of it as he could hear it in her heartbeats. He went down while she laid there curling her legs and biting her lips.

She pulled a pillow and covered her face as he took off his shirt. He leaned down and ran his finger over her thighs whilst pulling out the dress slowly. She still had her face covered.

He curled his legs around hers and leaned to kiss her lips. He tried pulling the pillow, but she didn't let go.

"*What happened?*" He murmured slowly as he tried to kiss her again, but she didn't let the pillow off it. He tried again slowly with his tender touch. "*Fuck me Anshit.*" She whispered tenuously.

He was taken aback, he wasn't sure if he heard it correct.

"*Hey, Kanishk*" he started when she interrupted abruptly.

"*Fuck me Anshit, fuck me harder than anyone would ever.*" She screamed, with her face still wrapped with a pillow. He was dumbstruck at that moment. He had no idea what was going on, but he knew it wasn't right.

He slid to the side and held her hand with which she had wrapped her face with the pillow. He removed it slowly.

He just stared at her, her eyes wet, tears running down on her cheek. He didn't say anything, he just laid there holding her hand, looking at her eyes. She had beautiful eyes which spoke a lot. It had a lot of stories buried deep down.

He wrapped her in a sheet and held her hands whilst she rested her head on his shoulders. She was crying continuously, he just stayed there holding her; for sometimes you just need people to let everything out, every tear that they have kept locked inside their heart.

He brewed some coffee as they sat again in the balcony. They sat there holding hands, watching the sky above turn dark blue.

"*I am sorry, I didn't tell you I am married.*" She murmured slowly as he saw her drop another tear.

"*I can leave if you want.*" She added as she looked at him.

He held her and wrapped his arms around her. Yes, it came as a surprise to him, but he remained calm. He knew it wasn't the perfect time to talk about it, so he avoided asking anything.

He held her tightly and comforted her. "*Don't worry, it doesn't matter to me.*"

"*Tell me whatever you have, you don't have to keep it buried inside.*" He said her as he brushed her hands gently.

She leaned slowly toward him, with her head resting on his shoulders. They sipped down the hot coffee together watching the far-off skyscrapers and some miniature red lights flickering over them.

She told him everything about her marriage, her husband's affairs, the pictures she saw, him being away almost every night lately.

He listened to everything she said. He was surprised to know such a horrific tale about her marriage. She was young, passionate, and beautiful. He held her hands and told her that it was the time for her to start living for herself and not for someone else. He told her how beautiful she was, and she blushed with every word he said. He made her realise that life was not meant to live for broken bits and pieces, it's about living it to the fullest no matter how difficult it is to start all over again. He held her hands and told her that she was too young to give up on her life, it had barely started. He made her believe that there is a new beginning waiting for her, she just needs to have the courage to go for it.

They sat there talking about everything until they realised it was already dawn. The saw the sky turning red and they could hear birds chirping away.

"*Come, I will take you somewhere.*" He said as he got up and walked inside the hall.

She came inside following him. "*Where?*" She asked.

"*You will get to know*" He replied.

"*Do you want to change into something comfortable?*" He asked as he saw her still wrapped in a sheet.

She changed into one of his tee and shorts and then they drove off. It was a beautiful morning. The road was lined up with yellow lights complimenting perfectly with the red sky. The sky was fading to new shades with every moment.

They drove off to the Marine Drive. Anshit parked the car, and then they walked towards the shore. The sky was fading to orange.

They sat there underneath the colourful sky, holding each other's hand.

"*Thanks for understanding everything.*" She said as she locked her fingers in his.

He kissed her forehead.

"*And by the way, I will be filing for divorce today.*" She said with a smile. He looked at her, her face was brimming with happiness as the first ray of sun fell over.

He smiled back looking into her eyes. She leaned forward and pulled him, they kissed while the sun rose from the horizon. It was a new morning for them, and a new morning for her life. They just kissed each other, and it felt like forever.

A LETTER FROM THE AUTHOR

Well, since you are here I am assuming you have already read the book, so first of all "Thank you!"

For those who got to know me through this book, this is actually a second version of the book. During Covid amid quarantine I wrote the first version and published it on Kindle. It had three stories whereas this published paperback version has five. It has been more than five years since I wrote the kindle version.

Just recently, a few weeks before I signed up with the publisher I was sitting with few of my close friends and we were talking about quite a few things over some drinks, about life, love, relationships and our shelved plans and passions. That's when the conversation broke about my writings and the fact that I have been writing for years, or I would say been trying to, but never got myself published, and it somewhere made me realise that I have to take the first step somewhere and see what awaits next.

And well, the very next morning I started working on this version of the book. I literally put continuous hours, working till the morning, clicking keys on my mac, re-reading and editing them and meanwhile also started reaching out to publishers.

So, yeah, it all happened like that and somewhere I am glad about that night which made me give it one more chance, a real one.

Fun fact, I have a whole novel which I wrote back in 2018 still in my drafts, which I just might look onto next. This is my first step towards years of longing and working but I am glad it is finally here.

Well, I will be ending my note here. I hope you liked my work, if yes, do let me know by any means of communication, socials or email, I would love to hear from you about my work.

Thank you!